Little Women

Louisa M. Alcott

Simplified by Michael West

1,500 word vocabulary

LONGMAN

LONGMAN GROUP UK LIMITED
Longman House
Burnt Mill, Harlow, Essex
CM20 2JE, England
and Associated Companies throughout world.

This edition © Longman Group Ltd 1957 & 1965

All rights reserved; no part of this publication may be
reproduced, stored in a retrieval system, or transmitted
in any form or by any means, electronic, mechanical,
photocopying, recording, or otherwise, without the prior
written permission of the Publishers.

First published in this series 1957
Second edition 1965
Thirty-first impression 1987

ISBN 0-582-53489-5

Note: Words outside stage 4 of the New Method Supple-
mentary Readers and are not explained in the text. These
extra words are in a list on page 121.

This edition is based on Miss Alcott's
Little Women and *Good Wives*

Produced by Longman Group (FE) Ltd
Printed in Hong Kong

Acknowledgements
We are grateful to the BBC for allowing us to use copyright photographs
from their production of Little Women by Louisa M. Acott. Jo played by
Angela Down; Meg played by Jo Rowbottom; Amy played by Janina Faye;
Beth played by Sarah Craze; Laurie played by Stephen Turner; Mr March
played by Patrick Troughton; John Brooke played by Martin Jarvis;
Professor Bhaer played by Frederick Jaeger.

Contents

Chapter		Page
1	The Four Sisters	1
2	Christmas Day	4
3	Meg and Jo	7
4	The Laurence Boy	8
5	Visit to Laurie	13
6	Beth Gets her Wish	18
7	A Quarrel	22
8	A Visit to Rich People	27
9	"All Play and No Work"	36
10	Dreamland	43
11	The Telegram	47
12	Illness	51
13	Life or Death?	59
14	The Mother's Return	63
15	That Bad Boy	66
16	A Happy Christmas	72
17	Jo and Meg	78
18	Meg, John Brooke and Aunt March	80
19	The End of the Year	86
20	The Little House	91
21	Growing Up	94
22	Jo in New York	98
23	Jo and Laurie	101
24	A Parting	103
25	Beth's Secret	105
26	A Meeting at Nice	108
27	Laurie and Amy	111
28	All Alone	115
29	A Homecoming	117
30	Under the Umbrella	119
	List of Extra Words	121

Meg 16 anni

Jo 15 anni

Beth 13 anni

Amy 12 anni

One

THE FOUR SISTERS

It was near Christmas-time. Four girls sat by a warm fire. They looked through the window at the snow falling outside.

"Christmas won't be Christmas without any presents," said Jo.

"Being poor makes one so unhappy!" said Meg, looking down at her old dress.

"I don't think it's fair that some girls should have pretty things and we should not," said Amy.

"We've got father and mother . . ." began Beth.

"We haven't got father, and we shan't have him for a long time," answered Jo.

These four sisters, who did not like being poor, lived in the town of Concord in the United States of America. At this time there was a war between the North and the South, and their father was away with the Army helping to take care of the sick and wounded. He had once been rich but had lost most of his money in trying to help a friend.

Meg—the eldest, could remember when there was plenty of money for everything that was needed. She was now sixteen years old and very pretty, with light brown hair, large eyes, small hands and feet. Her fifteen-year-old sister, Jo, was tall, thin and not very graceful. Jo had grey eyes and very lovely red-brown hair. She always wished she was a boy so she did not care how she looked. She loved to run and climb trees, and do things which boys like doing.

Beth was thirteen years old, bright-eyed, with a face like a rose. She was gentle and thoughtful, but was afraid of talking to people whom she did not know. In this she was very unlike her youngest sister, Amy. Amy was only twelve years old; she thought that she was an important person and was very proud of her golden hair, her white skin and blue eyes. She knew that her nose was rather flat; but she hoped to grow up to be beautiful and to marry a rich husband.

The girls' mother, Mrs. March, was giving all her time to working for the soldiers, making them warm clothes; and the girls had given up their Christmas presents for the soldiers. That was why Jo said: "Christmas won't be Christmas without any presents."

"Mother will be coming soon," said Beth.

She put her mother's shoes to warm in front of the fire; then Jo held them up close to it so as to warm them quickly.

"These shoes are quite worn out," she said. "Mother must have new ones."

"I have got a dollar, I thought that I would buy some for her with that," said Beth.

"No! I shall," cried Amy.

Jo stood up: "Father called me the 'man of the family' and told me to take special care of mother. So I will buy the shoes."

"Let us each get her something for Christmas," said Beth, "and not get anything for ourselves."

Jo began to march up and down with her hands behind her back, like a man.

"We will let her think that we are getting things for ourselves, and then surprise her," she said.

*

"I was so busy that I could not come home to dinner," said Mrs. March as she came in.

She took off her wet clothes and sat down by the fire.

Meg and Jo set ready the table for their evening meal. Beth was busy in the kitchen. Amy sat with her hands by her side and gave orders to everyone but did nothing herself.

When they were all sitting round the fire, Mrs. March said, "I have something nice for you girls— a letter."

"A letter from Father!" cried Jo. "How I wish I could be a soldier and go to help in the War."

"I don't," said Amy. "I should think it would be very unpleasant."

"When is he coming home?" asked Beth.

"Not for a very long time unless he is ill," replied their mother. "Now come and hear what your father writes to you."

It was a long letter, and the last part of it was written for the girls. "Give them my love," Mr. March wrote to his wife. "Tell them how much I think of them and pray for them. It will be a whole year before I shall see them; tell them not to waste the time, but to work hard. I know that they will be loving children to you and will do their duty. I hope that each one will try to fight against her own weakness, so that when I come back I may be proud of my little women."

Two

CHRISTMAS DAY

It was Christmas morning. The girls dressed quickly and went down to the sitting-room. There they met Hannah, the old servant who had lived with the family since Meg was born. Hannah was loved by them all, more as a friend than a servant.

"Where is Mother?" asked Meg.

"Someone came to call her to help a family who have no food," said Hannah.

"Oh well," said Meg, "you bring our breakfast and she will soon be back."

By the time Hannah had finished cooking, the girls were very hungry. Just at that minute their mother came in.

"Happy Christmas," they said.

"Happy Christmas, my daughters," said Mrs. March. "Before we sit down I want to tell you that I have just been to a house where there are six children. Their mother—Mrs. Hummel—has no fire to keep them warm and no food to give them. Hannah and I will take them some wood. Will you come with us and take them your breakfasts?"

They were all silent for a few minutes. Then Jo said, "What a good thing we hadn't begun to eat."

"May I go and help carry the things to the poor little children?" asked Beth eagerly.

"I shall take the hot cakes," said Amy, bravely giving up the food which she most liked.

Meg was already putting the bread and butter into a basket.

"I thought that you would do it," said Mrs. March, smiling. "You shall all go and help me, and when we come back we will have bread and milk for breakfast. We shall eat more at dinner-time so there will be no real loss."

In the evening they acted a play which Jo had written and a few friends came in to see it.

The play went well: the actors made a great deal of noise, and their friends who were listening shouted and laughed. Just as it was ending Hannah came into the room and said, "Mrs. March wants you all to come down and eat something."

This was not expected, even by the actors: and when they saw the table, they looked at one another with delighted surprise. There were cakes of all sorts; there was fruit, and sweets. It was a wonderful supper. In the middle of the table there was a pot of beautiful flowers.

"Where did it come from?" they all wanted to know.

"Did the fairies bring it?" asked Amy.

"Father Christmas brought it," said Beth.

"Mother did it," said Meg.

"Aunt March felt good for once, and sent us these things," said Jo.

"You are all wrong. Old Mr. Laurence in the big house next door sent it," replied Mrs. March.

"The Laurence boy's grandfather!" said Meg. "Why did he do that? We don't know him."

"Hannah told one of his servants that you took your breakfast to the poor children. He is rather a strange old gentleman, but that pleased him. He knew my father many years ago; and this afternoon he sent me a friendly note: 'I have heard what your children did this morning,' he wrote, 'and I am sending a little Christmas present to them.' So you have this nice meal to make up for a breakfast of bread and milk."

"I suppose it was his grandson who told him to do it," said Jo. "I think his grandson would like to get to know us, and I am sure that I should like to know him."

"I like his manners," said Mrs. March, "and I do not mind your knowing him when a proper chance comes. He brought the flowers himself; he looked very sad when he went away—hearing your fun and not having any of his own."

"We will have another play some time," said Jo.

"Perhaps he will help act in it. How good that would be!"

Three

MEG AND JO

The week after Christmas was a free time for the four sisters, especially for Meg and Jo, who had each found some work to do when their father lost his money. Meg went every day to teach Mrs. King's four little girls. She did not like this work, but she did it as well as she could, because she wished to help her family. Jo spent each day with her father's rich aunt a difficult old lady who lived in a large house nearby. Jo made herself useful by doing any of the things her aunt wanted—looking after her dog and her bird, helping to clean things and reading to her aunt in the afternoon. She did not like the books she read to her aunt; but she was sometimes able to go and find other books which she liked.

Betch was at home all the time, helping Hannah. Before her father went away she did her lessons with him, but now she did them by herself. Mrs. March had tried to send her to school, but she was too frightened to learn among a lot of other children. She loved music, and she prayed for a new piano instead of the old one in which many of the notes did not sound. Amy played a little, but she was proudest of her drawing, and she wanted to paint famous pictures when she grew up.

One day, Meg went over the house looking for Jo. She found her in the little room at the top of the house which was only used for storing things not wanted. Here Jo was lying on an old bed, reading and eating apples, while a friendly mouse came to sit beside her. The mouse ran into his hole when Meg came in with a letter.

"Such fun!" she said. "Sallie Gardiner's mother has asked us to a little dance tomorrow, and Mother says that we may go. Now, what *shall* we wear?"

"What's the use of asking that, when you know that we have only one dress each that we can wear?" said Jo.

Four

THE LAURENCE BOY

On the next afternoon the sisters began to get ready for the dance, and at last, with the help of Beth and Amy, they were ready.

As soon as they arrived, Meg began to enjoy herself. Her friend Sallie looked after her, and several young men asked her to dance. Meg danced beautifully, even though her pretty shoes hurt her. She was proud of her small feet, and sometimes she bought shoes that were not big enough.

Jo sat quietly looking across at some boys who were laughing and talking about skating: she loved skating. Jo generally liked talking to boys better than to girls; but she knew that she must not go over to join them. When a young man came towards her to ask her to dance, Jo went behind the door to escape. To her surprise she found a boy in the passage.

"I didn't expect to find anyone here," she said, preparing to go out again as quickly as she came in.

But the boy laughed and said pleasantly, "Don't mind me; stay if you like."

"Shan't I trouble you?"

"Not a bit; I only came out here because I don't know many people, and I felt rather strange at first, you know."

"So did I. Don't go away, please, unless you'd rather."

The boy sat down again. He sat silent, looking at his shoes. At last, trying to be pleasant and easy, Jo said, "I think I have seen you before; you live near us, don't you?"

"Next door," and he looked up and laughed.

Jo laughed too, and said, "We did have such a good time with your nice Christmas present."

"My grandfather sent it."

"But you told him to, didn't you, Mr. Laurence?"

"What makes you think that, Miss March?"

"I'm not Miss March; I'm only Jo."

"And I'm not Mr. Laurence; I'm only Laurie."

"Laurie Laurence—what a strange name!"

"My first name is Theodore, but I don't like it, for the fellows called me Dora, so I made them say Laurie instead."

"I hate my name too—Josephine, and I wish everyone would call me Jo. How did you make the boys stop calling you Dora?"

"I hit them."

"I can't hit Aunt March, so I suppose I shall have to bear it," said Jo.

They watched the dancing for a few minutes, and then Laurie said:

"Don't you like dancing, Miss Jo?"

"I like it well enough, if there is plenty of room. In a place like this I'm sure to step on people's feet, or do something wrong, so I keep out of it. Don't you dance?"

"Sometimes; but I've been away so long—at school in Italy and Switzerland and in Paris—that I don't know how things are done here."

Jo decided that she liked Laurie very much. She wondered how old he was, but did not like to ask.

"I suppose you will be going to college soon," she said. "I often see you working at your books."

"Not for a year or two," he replied. "I shall not go before I'm seventeen."

"Aren't you sixteen yet?" asked Jo, looking at the tall lad whom she thought must be seventeen already.

"Sixteen next month." And then, as the music began again, he said suddenly, "This is a lovely dance; won't you dance; won't you have it with me?"

"I can't: I told Meg I wouldn't, because—" There Jo stopped for a minute; but she decided to go on. "You see, the back of my dress is burnt and, although I put a piece in, it doesn't look very well. Meg told me to keep still, so that no one would see it. You may laugh if you want to; it is funny, I know."

But Laurie didn't laugh. He said very gently, "Never mind that; there is a long hall outside there, where we can dance with no one to see us. Please come."

How they enjoyed that dance together! When the music stopped, they sat down to get cool. They were just beginning to have a pleasant talk when someone came to tell Jo that Meg wished to see her. She had hurt her foot and was resting in a side room. Jo was sorry to leave Laurie, but she went at once.

She found Meg resting, with her foot on a chair. "I've hurt my foot," she said. "It turned over— I suppose because these shoes are too small. It hurts so much that I won't be able to walk home."

"I knew you'd hurt your feet with those silly little shoes," said Jo. "We will have to get a carriage. You can't stay here all night."

"A carriage would cost a lot of money; and I don't think we could get one. It is a long way from here to the town and we have no one to send."

"I'll go," said Jo.

"No! No! It's late and very dark," said Meg. "You can't go."

"I'll ask Laurie, and he will go," cried Jo.

"No! Don't ask anyone. I can't dance any more, but Hannah will soon come. Tell me as soon as you see her. They are going in now. You go and have something to eat and bring me some coffee."

Jo got the coffee but as she turned to carry it back she poured it down the front of her dress.

"Oh! Oh! Oh!" she cried. "Now I've spoilt

my dress!"

"Can I help you?" said a friendly voice. It was Laurie. He was carrying cakes in one hand and a cup of coffee in the other.

"I was trying to get something for Meg."

"And I was looking for someone to give this to."

Jo led him to Meg. Laurie brought more coffee and cakes for Jo and they sat down together. They were so happy that Meg forgot about her foot. When Hannah came she stood up quickly, but she soon sat down again in great pain. Laurie saw at once that she could not walk home.

"My grandfather's carriage has just come," he said. "Let me take you home in it."

"But are you going so early?" said Jo. "You don't want to go home yet!"

"Yes, I do. I always go early. Please let me take you all home."

Soon they were all on their way home in Mr. Laurence's large carriage. They said "good night" to Laurie with many thanks, and went in quietly, hoping not to wake their young sisters. But soon two little voices cried out—

"Tell us about the dance! Tell us about the dance!"

When the story had been told and the little girls were asleep again, Jo bathed Meg's foot and brushed her hair.

"I really feel like a fine young lady," said Meg; "I came home from the party in a carriage, and now I have a servant to brush my hair."

"I don't believe that fine young ladies enjoy themselves a bit more than we do," said Jo.

Perhaps Jo was right!

Five

VISIT TO LAURIE

One afternoon Jo came back early from Aunt March because it had been snowing heavily. She did not feel like sitting by the fire, so she took a brush and began to make a path through the snow so that Beth could walk through the garden. She watched old Mr. Laurence drive away from the house next door; and then, as she was brushing away the snow near the wall which separated the two houses, she saw an unhappy-looking Laurie through one of the windows.

"Poor Laurie," thought Jo, "he's all alone; he needs a lot of friends to make him happy."

She threw up a handful of snow against the window, and Laurie turned to see her. At once his face changed. He laughed, opened the window and called to her.

She shook her brush at him as she called out, "Are you ill?"

Laurie opened the window and said in a thick voice, "I've had a cold, and have been in my bedroom for a week, but I'm better now."

"What do you find to do?"

"Nothing! Grandfather reads to me, but I don't like the books he reads."

"Why don't you get someone to come up?"

"I don't know anyone. Won't you come?"

"I will if Mother will let me. I'll go and ask her. Shut that window, and wait till I come."

Jo came back in a few minutes, and was taken up to Laurie's room by a servant.

"Mother sent you her love," she said when she entered Laurie's room; "and Meg sent you this cake for your tea."

"How kind you all are," said Laurie.

"Shall I read to you?" asked Jo.

"No, I would much rather you talked. Tell me about your sisters. Beth is the one who stays at home, isn't she, and Meg is the pretty one, and Amy is the little girl?"

"How did you know?" Jo asked.

"Well," said Laurie, "I often hear you calling each other, and you always seem to be having such fun. I know that it is not right to look through people's windows; but sometimes it is like looking at a picture. I see you all in the firelight, sitting round the table with your mother. I haven't any mother, you know."

He looked so sad that Jo cried, "You may look as much as you like. But why don't you come and see us? Wouldn't your grandfather allow you?"

"He would if your mother asked me. He lives very much with his books. My teacher, Mr. Brooke, doesn't live here in the house, so I haven't anyone to go out with, and I stay at home most of the time."

"That's bad for you," said Jo. "You ought to

go out more."

"Do you like your school?" asked Laurie.

"I don't go to school. I go to look after my difficult old aunt."

Jo talked about her aunt's fat little dog and the bird, and the books which she had to read to her aunt; and she made Laurie laugh till the tears ran down his face.

Then they began talking of books.

"If you like them so much," said Laurie, "go down and see ours. Grandfather is out, so you needn't be afraid."

"I'm not afraid of anything."

"I don't believe you are," said Laurie. He was afraid sometimes; he was rather afraid of his solemn old grandfather. He took Jo down to a large room filled with books and pictures. Jo looked round the room: "What a lot of books!" she said. Just at that moment the bell rang and one of the servants came in and said, "The doctor has come to see Laurie."

"Do you mind if I leave you for a few minutes?" he said.

"Of course not. I'm so happy with all these things to look at."

Jo stood for some time before a fine picture of old Mr. Laurence, and when the door opened she said to Laurie, "I'm sure I shouldn't be afraid of him. He has kind eyes, even if his mouth is hard. Of course he's not as good-looking as my grandfather, but I like him."

"Thank you, madam," said a deep voice; and Jo turned to find—not Laurie—but old Mr. Laurence himself.

For a minute she thought she must run away; but, as she looked at the old man, she saw that he was smiling.

"So you're not afraid of me," he said.

"Not much, sir."

"And I am not so good-looking as your mother's father?"

"Not quite, sir."

"But you like me?"

"Yes, I do, sir," said Jo.

That answer pleased the old gentleman. He laughed, shook hands with her and said:

"You are brave, like your grandfather, my dear. What have you been doing to my grandson?"

"Only trying to be good neighbours. He is all alone, and we girls would like to help him if we can, because we haven't forgotten your Christmas present."

"How are the poor little children to whom you gave your breakfast?"

"The Hummels? They are doing well, sir."

"Tell your mother I shall come over to see her soon; and now let us go in to tea."

At this minute Laurie came running in. He was very surprised to see Jo and his grandfather talking together; and the old man was equally surprised, during tea, to hear Laurie and Jo talking like two old friends.

"How happy he is!" he thought. "She has done

him good already."

After tea, Laurie took Jo over the large house, showing her all the lovely things in it. When they went back to old Mr. Laurence, Jo looked at the big piano. How she wished that Beth could see it!

"Do you play, Laurie?" said Jo.

"Sometimes," he replied.

"His music is not bad," said his grandfather, "but I hope he will do well in more important things." Jo stood up to go. "Must you go?" he asked.

"Yes, sir; it's late."

"Come again," said Laurie.

"Yes," said Jo, "if you promise to come and see us when your cold is better."

"Indeed, I will," said Laurie.

Six

BETH GETS HER WISH

After Jo's visit, a new life began for Laurie. Mrs. March was glad to see him whenever he wished to come to the house, and soon he and the four girls were the greatest friends. Laurie spent less time on his lessons, but old Mr. Laurence was pleased to see him happy in the company of people of his own age. There were evening parties in the big house, and Laurie and the girls arranged plays and out-of-door parties together.

Meg liked wandering over the large house. Jo liked to sit for hours in the big room reading, and Amy looked at the pictures. Only Beth was too afraid to enter the house. She wanted to play the big piano, but she feared old Mr. Laurence too much to go near him.

When Mr. Laurence discovered this, he tried to make it easy for Beth to come. One day, when he was visiting Mrs. March and the four girls, he began to talk about music and musicians, until the music-loving Beth came nearer and nearer to his chair to listen. Then he went on to talk of Laurie's music lessons.

"Laurie hasn't much time for his music now," he said; and then, as though the thought had just come to him, he went on, "I am glad of this, for I did not want him to spend so much time upon it; but the piano should be used, and I do wish that some of your girls would come and play on it sometimes. They needn't see anyone, and they won't trouble me, for I shall be in my room at the other end of the house."

As he got up to go, he said, "Of course, if they don't care to come—"

Here Beth put her hand into his and said, "Oh, sir, I do care—I care very much."

"Are you the musical girl?"

"I'm Beth, and I do love music. I'll come, if you're sure no one will hear me."

"No one, my dear—come as often as you like." He held out his hand; and Beth, no longer afraid, put her small hand trustfully in his, for she had no

20

words to thank him for his kindness.

Early next morning, Beth watched old Mr.
Laurence go out and then she set off for the big
house. After twice turning back in fear, she at last
went in by a side-door and made her way as
quietly as she could to the room where the piano
was. Laurie had left some easy but very pretty
music for her, and she spent a delightful morning
playing it on the great piano. She forgot her fears,
herself, and everything else except the pleasure
which the music gave her. At last Hannah came to
tell her the time, and take her home to dinner.

After that, Beth went to play on the piano every
morning. She never met anyone, and she never
knew that old Mr. Laurence often sat in his study
listening to her, and thinking of his dearly-loved
little granddaughter who died long ago. Beth was
so happy and so thankful that she decided to make
some shoes for old Mr. Laurence. With the help
of her mother and sisters over the difficult parts,
she soon finished them and sent them to him. For
two days there was no reply. Beth was afraid that
the old gentleman was not pleased with them. Then,
one morning, when she returned from a walk,
several joyful voices called out to her:

"Here's a letter for you, Beth. Come quick, and
read it!"

As Beth hurried in, Jo cried out, "Oh, Beth,
look at what he has sent you!" They were all
pointing and saying, "Look there! Look there!"

Beth did look, and turned white with delight,

for there stood a small piano, with a letter lying upon it for "Miss Elizabeth March." Beth opened and read it. It was a rather solemn letter, as if written to someone grown-up:

Miss March.
Dear Madam,

I have never had any shoes which pleased me so well as yours. I should like to return your kindness, and so I am sending you the small piano which was once used by my granddaughter.

With many thanks and best wishes.

I am, Your friend,
James Laurence.

All the girls gathered round to see the beautiful piano, while Beth sat down to try it. She found it perfect.

"Now you'll have to go and thank him," said Jo—half in fun, for she did not think that Beth would be brave enough.

"I am going now," said Beth, "before I get afraid." Then, to the surprise of everyone, she walked out of the house, down the garden path, and in at the Laurence's door, before they could believe what had happened.

Old Mr. Laurence looked very surprised to see her.

"I came to thank you, sir," she began; but she did not finish what she was saying, for he looked so friendly, and smiled so kindly at her, that she put both her arms round his neck and kissed him.

The old gentleman was pleased by the trusting little girl. He took her on his knee, and Beth was soon talking to him as if she had known him all her life. When she went home he walked with her to her own gate, shook hands, and lifted his hat.

When the girls saw this happen, Jo began to dance with joy, Amy nearly fell out of the window in her surprise, and Meg said, "Well, I do believe the world is coming to an end."

Seven

A QUARREL

It was Saturday afternoon. Amy was just getting better from a cold. She found her sisters dressing to go out, and asked them to tell her where they were going.

"Little girls shouldn't ask questions," said Jo.

This made Amy very angry.

"Do tell me, Meg," she said. "I think you might take me too. I am always left alone, because Beth spends so much time with her piano."

"I can't take you. You haven't been asked."

"Now, Meg," said Jo, "don't tell her. Amy can't go. She mustn't be a baby and be angry about it."

"I know you are going with Laurie to see the Fairy Play," said Amy, "and I *shall* go too. I've got a little money and I shall pay for myself."

"Just listen, Amy," said Meg. "Mother doesn't want you to go out so soon after your cold. You can go next week with Beth and Hannah."

"I shan't like that nearly as well as going with you and Laurie. Do take me, Meg! I'll be so good."

"Shall we take her, Jo?" asked Meg. "She could put on her warm clothes, and I don't believe that Mother would mind.

"No," replied Jo. "If she goes, I won't; and Laurie won't like that."

"I will go!" cried Amy.

"You couldn't sit with us," said Jo, "because we could not get another seat just next to ours. The seat would be somewhere else; but we couldn't let you sit alone, so you would have to have Laurie's seat, and then he would have to sit alone. So you must not come."

Amy began to cry, and Meg tried to make her understand. Then Laurie came. As the elder girls went away with him she called out, "You'll be sorry for this, Jo March."

This rather spoiled Jo's enjoyment of the play. She and Amy often had quarrels. Jo was always sorry that she had been angry after them. She knew that she had a very quick temper and she tried not to give way to it.

When they returned, Jo expected to find that Amy had done something to hurt her, but she did not find out what it was until the next afternoon. A few days before this, Jo had finished writing some little stories in a book; and she meant to give the book to her father.

"Have you seen my little book?" she asked the others.

"No," said Meg and Beth. Jo looked at Amy. "You've got it, Amy?"

"No, I haven't," said Amy. "I don't know where it is, and I don't care."

"You know something about it. Tell me at once, or I'll make you," said Jo, shaking her.

"You'll never see your silly book again," said Amy. "I burnt it."

"What? My little book that I worked so hard over, to give to father when he comes back! You couldn't burn my little book?"

"Yes, I did—I told you I'd make you pay for not taking me yesterday."

Jo shook Amy, shouting as she did so, "You bad, bad girl! I can never write it again, and I'll never forgive you."

Meg and Beth ran to save Amy; and Jo ran up to her little room at the top of the house and shut herself in to fight against her temper.

In the sitting-room Amy too was unhappy.

"How could you do such a thing?" said Meg.

Beth and her mother were too hurt to say much, and Amy felt that no one loved her.

Jo came down at tea-time, still looking so angry that Amy was hardly brave enough to say:

"Please forgive me, Jo. I'm very, very sorry."

"I shall never forgive you," replied Jo, and took no further notice of her for the rest of the evening.

When bed-time came, Mrs. March said to Jo, "My dear, don't let the sun go down on your anger. Forgive each other, help each other, and begin again tomorrow."

Jo felt like putting her head down and crying but she knew that Amy was listening, so she said, in a hard voice.

"It was a very bad thing to do, and I can never forgive her."

On the next afternoon, when Jo came back from a rather difficult morning with Aunt March, she still felt angry and unhappy.

"I'll ask Laurie to go skating on the ice with me," she said to herself. "He is so kind and friendly. He'll soon make me feel better."

Amy watched her go and said to Meg:

"She promised to take me skating next time she went, and this is the last ice we shall have; but it's no good asking her when she is so angry."

"Well, Amy, you were very unkind to burn her book, and it is hard for her to forgive you. But if you go after her now, you may find that Laurie has made her feel better. Tell her again that you are sorry, and perhaps she will be friends."

"I'll try," said Amy.

She put on her warm coat and ran off as quickly as she could. It was not far to the river, and both Jo and Laurie were ready before Amy reached them. Jo saw her coming and turned her back. Laurie did not see her. He was trying the ice a little further on. He called back to Jo:

"Keep near the side; the ice isn't safe in the middle."

Jo said to herself as she followed Laurie, "Did Amy hear that it isn't safe in the middle? Ought I to tell her?—No, let her take care of herself."

She decided to go on, but something held her. She turned round just in time to see Amy throw up her hands with a cry that made Jo's heart stand still with fear as Amy fell through the thin ice into the water.

Laurie lay on the ice, and held out his stick to Amy. Together they got her out, unhurt, but very cold and wet.

They took off their coats and put them round Amy to keep her warm.

"We must make her run as fast as she can, before she takes cold," said Laurie.

They all ran home, and very soon Amy was in a warm bed, with a fire in her room. Before long she was fast asleep.

Mrs. March and Jo went up to see her.

"Are you sure she is safe?" asked Jo.

"Quite safe. You and Laurie did the right thing, putting your coats on her and hurrying her back home."

"Oh, Mother," said Jo, weeping, "if she had died it would have been because of my wicked temper. I was angry with her and did not tell her to keep near the side. I know that I shall do something in a temper one day which will spoil my life. Oh, Mother, what shall I do? What shall I do?"

"You must try not to be angry with other people.

We all do things which make other people angry. Sometimes you do things which make me angry, but I hold myself back; I keep back the angry words and learn to understand and forgive. I have been learning that lesson for forty years."

"Oh, Mother, if only I could be half as good as you!" said Jo.

"I hope you will be a great deal better, my dear," replied her mother.

Jo held her mother close, and together they watched Amy. She moved in her sleep, woke with a smile, and held out her arms to Jo. In the kiss that followed, the sisters were friends again and their quarrel forgotten.

Eight

A VISIT TO RICH PEOPLE

Annie Moffat met Meg at Mrs. Gardiner's party and liked her: they became great friends.

In the spring Annie asked Meg and her friend, Sallie Gardiner, to stay at her home for two weeks. Meg was teaching four little girls; but they were ill, so Meg was able to go. Jo and Amy helped her to get her clothes ready for the visit.

"I think your old blue house-dress looks pretty now it has been made longer," said Beth.

"Your grey dress will do very well for the small parties, and you will have your white dress for the larger ones," said Jo.

"I think you look lovely in white," said Amy, touching the white dress with loving fingers.

Meg was not entirely happy: her white dress had been washed many times, and she knew that the Moffats were rich and had many clothes.

"I wonder if I shall ever be able to buy the new dresses I really want," she said.

"You once said that you would be happy if only you could go and stay with the Moffats," said Beth.

"So I did. I *am* happy, and I will try not to think how much I want just *one* new dress."

At last all the preparations were finished; the simple clothes were put in a travelling-case, and Meg set out on her journey.

She found that the Moffats were indeed rich, and that their house was large and full of costly things. Both Mr. and Mrs. Moffat were fat and happy-looking. They were pleasure-loving people; they loved money and what it could buy; but they were kind, and they wished to make Meg's visit happy. Meg enjoyed the lazy, care-free life, with plenty of time to arrange her hair, dress herself, and go out with others. In the daytime she was taken out in the carriage and in the evening they often went to see plays. Everyone seemed to love pretty Meg, and she was very happy. When she saw all the nice things that the Moffats had, she wanted to be rich, and as she looked back at her own home, she thought how small and poor it was.

During the second week a small party had been

arranged, at which Meg had expected to wear her simple grey dress. But she found that it would not do among the fine evening dresses of her friends; so she wore the white dress which she had meant to keep for the bigger party on the next night. Even this looked very poor by the side of the other dresses, and she knew from their looks, that the other girls thought so too.

When she was feeling very troubled about her dress, a servant brought in a large box and a letter. To everyone's surprise, both were for Meg. When the box was opened the girls saw the loveliest roses.

"What fun," said Annie, "we didn't know you had a lover."

"The letter is from my mother," said Meg, "and the roses are from Laurie."

After reading her mother's letter, Meg felt happy again. When the party began she danced and sang and was so happy that she looked even prettier than usual. She was enjoying every minute until she happened to hear Mrs. Moffat talking to her daughter Belle.

"How old is young Laurence?"

"About sixteen or seventeen."

"He would make a good husband for one of the March girls," said Mrs. Moffat. "He'll be quite rich when his grandfather dies. I expect Mrs. March is making her plans, although it is so early. Clearly the girl doesn't think of it yet."

"Poor girl!" replied Belle. "She has only that one old white dress; do you think we might offer to lend her another? She's very proud, but perhaps she wouldn't mind."

"We'll see," said Mrs. Moffat. "I shall ask young Laurence to come to the party tomorrow."

Meg was very angry when she heard her mother spoken of like this. For the first time she began to understand how other people might think of Laurie's friendship with herself and her sisters, and she felt unhappy too that these people should think like this about her old dress. She hid her feelings, however, and no one knew what she had heard.

The next morning Belle Moffat said to her, "Mother has asked Mr. Laurence to the party tonight."

"He won't come," said Meg, laughing.

"Why?"

"He's too old; he's over seventy."

"Of course we mean the young man."

"There isn't a young man. Laurie is only a boy."

"But he's nearly your age," said Belle.

"Oh no," said Meg. "He's only about fifteen, and I'm nearly seventeen."

"It's very nice of him to send you flowers."

"Yes, he often does—to all of us—because there are so many in his house, and we love them so."

Just then Mrs. Moffat came into the room and asked what the girls were going to wear for the big party that night.

"I shall wear my red silk," said Sallie. "What are you going to wear, Meg?" she asked.

"My white one again," said Meg, "although it

got rather dirty last night."

"Why don't you send home for another?"

"Because I haven't another," said Meg.

"Only one dress? How strange!" said Sallie; but she did not finish because Belle Moffat shook her head at Sallie, and said kindly:

"There is no need for Meg to have a lot of dresses. She is not really old enough to go to many parties yet. As it happens, Meg," she went on, "there is a blue dress of mine which is too small for me, and I should love you to wear it."

"You are very kind," said Meg, "but I don't mind my old dress if you don't. It does well enough for a little girl like me."

"Oh, do wear it, Meg, and do let me help you to get ready for the party. You're so pretty; I should love to dress you without telling the others, and then show them what a real beauty you are. Please do, Meg!"

Meg did not like to say "No" to such a kind offer, and she wanted very much to see how she would look dressed in a really grown-up dress. She therefore decided to forget her former feelings about the Moffats, and promised to do as Belle wished.

That evening Belle and the French servant, Hortense, shut themselves in Meg's room and set to work on her. They powdered her face, neck and arms; they waved her hair. Then they put on the blue dress which was so small in places that it hurt her, and was so low at the neck that she felt undressed. Then they put on jewellery and ear-rings.

She had high blue shoes and she carried her flowers in a silver holder.

Belle and Hortense were delighted. "Come and show yourself," they said.

"I feel both over-dressed and undressed," said Meg. She did indeed look very pretty, but her dress was not right for so young a girl, and many people at the party asked who she was. Just as she was talking with a group of young men she saw Laurie. He bowed to her, but looked so surprised that she wished she had worn her old white dress.

"I'm glad you came," she said.

"Jo wanted me to come, to tell her how you looked."

"What will you tell her?"

"I shall say that I did not know you: you looked so grown-up and unlike yourself."

"The girls dressed me up for fun. Don't you like my dress?"

"I do not," said Laurie.

"Why not?"

"I do not like that sort of dress, and I don't think it is right for you."

"You are the unkindest boy I ever knew," said Meg, and turned away, only to hear one of the older men say, "They are making a fool of that little girl. She looked so sweet last night, but now they have made her a painted doll."

"Oh!" thought Meg, "I wish I'd been wiser and worn my own dress, even if it is old."

Laurie came back and asked her to dance. "I don't like your dress," he said, "but I like you."

Meg smiled and stood up with him.

"Take care you don't fall over my long dress—I know I was silly to wear it."

They had often danced together at home, and in the pleasure of the dance they forgot their little quarrel. They both danced well and were very happy.

"Promise me that you won't tell them at home about my dress. It would trouble mother."

Laurie promised. Just then Ned Moffat came to ask Meg to dance. Laurie watched them, and after the dance he was surprised to see Meg drink several glasses of wine. He went across and said to her, "Don't drink much of that, Meg."

"I'm not Meg tonight," she said with a laugh. "I'm a different girl in this dress."

When the next dance came, the wine had "gone to her head" and she danced faster and faster. Later, she was talking and laughing rather loud with a group of young men. Laurie was very unhappy about her, but he had no chance of speaking to her again before the party ended and he had to go home.

The next morning Meg had such a bad head that she stayed in bed, and on the following day, when her visit ended, she was rather glad to go home.

After the journey back, she sat with her mother and Jo in the evening, looking round at the little room.

"Home is a nice place," she said, "and it is so pleasant to be quiet."

"I'm glad to hear you say so. I thought you might not think so," said her mother, who had a feeling, as she listened to Meg's story, that something was troubling her daughter.

"Mother, there is something else which I must tell you," said Meg.

"Shall I go?" asked Jo.

"Of course not," said Meg. "You know that I tell you everything."

"We are waiting," said her mother, smiling but a little troubled.

"Well, I told you they dressed me up, but I didn't tell you how they made me look. Laurie did not like my dress. I heard one man call me a 'painted doll'. I know it was silly, but I wanted, for once, to see how it felt to be dressed like that. Then the boys gave me some wine and that made me even more silly. I am so sorry, Mother."

"Is that all, Meg?" asked her mother. "I think there is still something more which is troubling you."

"Yes," said Meg, and she went on to tell what Mrs. Moffat had said about Laurie. "She said that you were making plans for him to marry one of us because he will be rich."

Mrs. March looked very angry. Jo cried out at once, "I never heard anything so silly. Just wait till I see the Moffats! And won't Laurie laugh when he hears you want him to marry one of us!"

"If you tell Laurie, I shall never forgive you," said Meg. "She must not tell him, Mother!"

"No, Jo," said Mrs. March. "You must never

tell such foolish things. I ought not to have let you go to stay there, Meg. The Moffats may be kind, but they think more of money than of anything else. I hope that your visit there has not been bad for you."

"I enjoyed part of it very much—it was such fun! But I've learnt a great deal—among other things I know now how silly I was." Then she went on: "But do you make plans for us, Mother?"

"Yes, my dear, like all mothers, I make plans, but not the ones Mrs. Moffat spoke about. You and Jo are both old enough to know what I want for you. Of course I want you to be beautiful and good; and I want you to marry and be happy, because the best thing for any girl is to be happily married. It is right to think of it, Meg; right to hope for it; and wise to prepare for it, so that when the time comes you may be a good and happy wife. But I do not want you to marry rich men just because they are rich and can give you large houses and other good things. I would rather see you poor men's wives, if you are happy and loved."

Nine

"ALL PLAY AND NO WORK"

After Meg returned, the four girls began to enjoy the spring. They went for long walks, gathering wild flowers; they worked in the garden, where each had a part to herself, planting it with whatever flowers she liked. They went in a boat on the river with Laurie; in fact Laurie took part in most of the things which they did. On rainy days they wrote for the little weekly newspaper, put together by Jo, which Meg read aloud to them in Jo's top room every Saturday night. After a time, Laurie was allowed to write for this newspaper, and to be present at the Saturday night readings.

It was because of this that he thought of making the old bird-house into a post-office. It was near the wall separating the gardens and could be used by both families. They "posted" all sorts of things to each other—poems and garden-seeds, music, letters and cakes. Even old Mr. Laurence joined in the fun and sent unexpected presents, while his gardener, who was very friendly with old Hannah, sent her a love letter. How they all laughed! Beth was the postman for the March family, and they all enjoyed the fun of having their own post-office.

Soon the spring ended and it was summer. One warm day in June, Meg came back from her work and called to the others:

"The King children are going away tomorrow for three months at the sea. So I am free! I have no work for three months. How I shall enjoy it!"

She found Jo equally happy, but very tired after preparing her aunt's clothes and seeing her off for a long stay in the country.

"What will you do with your free time?" asked Amy.

"I shall stay in bed late in the mornings," replied Meg, "and then get up and do nothing—nothing but rest all day."

"I would not like that," said Jo. "I have brought back plenty of books, and I shall read, and read—that is, when I'm not having fun."

"Don't let us do any lessons, Beth," said Amy.

"If Meg and Jo do nothing but play and rest, we ought to do the same."

"Well, I will, if Mother doesn't mind. I want to learn some new music and I must make some summer clothes for my dolls."

"May we all be really free, Mother," asked Meg, "and just do nothing but what we like?"

"You may try your plan for a week, and see how you like it. I think that, by the end of the week, you will be very tired of all play and no work."

"Oh no," said Meg. "I shall love it."

The next morning Meg came down late to breakfast. She did not enjoy eating it alone, and the room was dirty because Beth had not cleaned it. Amy had left her books lying about. Jo had not changed the flowers. Only her mother's corner of the room looked as usual.

Meg sat dreaming of the pretty dresses she would like to buy. Jo had gone out after breakfast to spend the morning on the river with Laurie. Beth left the breakfast things for Hannah to wash and went to look for something from which to make dolls' clothes. When she was tired of this she left all the things on the floor and went to her piano.

Amy put on her best white dress and sat in the garden. When she got tired of doing nothing she went for a walk and was caught in the rain, which spoilt her dress.

In the evening the girls told their mother how much they had enjoyed the day, but Mrs. March did not think that they looked very happy. All that week their work was done by Hannah and Mrs. March, and so the house was well looked after, while Meg sat trying to make her clothes look like Annie Moffat's, and Jo read until her eyes were tired, and she quarrelled with everyone—even with Laurie. Amy was the most unhappy, because she found that, without Meg and Jo to help her, she had nothing to do except draw, and she soon grew tired of that. Beth sometimes forgot that she was supposed to be lazy, and she went on with some of her usual work, but even she was less peaceful and happy than usual.

On the last day of the week Mrs. March decided to give the girls a lesson. When they came down in the morning there was no breakfast, and the kitchen fire had not been lighted. Meg went upstairs to see what was the matter.

"I am not ill," said Mrs. March. "Hannah and I are very tired, so I have given Hannah a day's rest and I shall stay quietly in my room and go out later for a walk. You will have to do without us."

Jo was pleased to have something to do. She and Meg prepared the breakfast and took some to their mother. The tea was badly made and the eggs were hard, but Mrs. March only smiled. She had taken some food up before, knowing what sort of breakfast the girls might bring, but she did not let them see that she did not eat what they had brought.

"They are going to have a hard day, but it will do them good," she thought.

Meg was not at all pleased with the way she had cooked the breakfast, so Jo offered to get the dinner. Remembering her quarrel with Laurie, she thought she would ask him to dinner and make friends again.

"You had better see what there is before you ask any friends," said Meg.

"Oh, there's plenty of meat and green stuff, and I shall get some fish and some fruit, and make some coffee."

"Don't try too many things, Jo. You can't really cook anything but sweets, and you had better ask Mother before you buy anything."

"Of course I shall," said Jo, going to Mrs. March's room. Her mother looked up from her book and said, "Buy what you like. I shall be going out to dinner later on."

Jo could hardly believe it was her mother sitting in a chair reading so early in the morning.

"Nothing seems right this morning," she said to herself. "There's Beth crying—that is always a sign that there is something wrong with this family."

She hurried down to find Beth crying as though her heart would break. Her little bird, Pip, was lying dead. His food box was empty and there was no water.

"I made him die," cried Beth. "I forgot to feed him. Oh, Pip, how could I be so unkind?"

Jo picked up the little bird and found it quite dead.

"I'll never, never have another bird," cried Beth.

"I'm too bad to have one."

Jo would have liked to stay with Beth, but she had so much to do that she had to leave her to the others and go back to the kitchen to "wash up." Here she found that the water was cold, as the fire had not been lighted. It took some time to light it, and she decided that it would be best to go out to buy the food while waiting for the water to get hot. She bought some fish—but not enough for the party, and some not very good fruit. She found that she did not know much about buying food.

Meg had promised to make the bread but she sat talking to her friend, Sallie Gardiner, and forgot.

Jo opened the door. "Did you remember the bread?"

"Oh! I'll make it now," said Meg.

She made it hurriedly, so it was heavy and burnt.

Miss Crocker was an old lady whom they tried to help; but no one liked her. She arrived to dinner just after Mrs. March had gone out for a walk; so Meg had to sit and talk to her while Jo cooked the dinner. There were so many things to do! The meat had to be cooked—and the fish; and the fruit had to be prepared, and the table had to be set ready.

At last Jo rang the bell. The dinner was nearly an hour late. Poor Jo! Everything had gone wrong. The meat was cooked too much; the fish was cooked too little and there was not enough of it; and the bread was black.

Amy laughed; Miss Crocker looked angry and

Meg looked hurt. Only Laurie was kind, and talked and laughed as though he was enjoying his dinner.

"Well," thought Jo, "the fruit will be good, because I put plenty of sugar on it and we have cream to put on it."

Miss Crocker tasted it first, and quickly drank some water. Laurie ate his bravely without saying a word; then Amy, who had taken rather a lot, began to cry out. She got up quickly and ran from the table.

"What is it?" asked Jo.

"You put salt instead of sugar," said Meg, "and the cream is bad because you forgot to put it in the ice-box."

Jo's face was very red and she was nearly crying. When she looked at Laurie she saw that he was trying not to laugh. Quite suddenly she laughed too—laughed until the tears ran down her face. So did all the others, even Miss Crocker.

Meg helped Jo to clear the table, and to "wash up" and clean the kitchen, while Laurie took Amy for a drive. They were so tired that they did not wish to do any more work that day, but as there were friends coming to tea they had to hurry to be ready.

When Mrs. March came back she found the three girls still working. They were not able to sit down and rest until late in the evening.

"What a very bad day!" said Jo to her mother.

"Not a bit like home," put in Amy.

"Not without you," said Beth, putting her arms round her mother.

"Well, girls," said Mrs. March, "are you pleased

with this week, and do you want another week like it?"

"I don't," said Jo.

"Nor I," said the others.

"You think, then, that it is better to have a few duties, and to work for the others?"

"I'm tired of this week," said Jo. "I mean to begin work again."

"Suppose you learn to cook," said her mother. "Every girl ought to learn that," she added, smiling, for she had met Miss Crocker and heard about Jo's dinner.

"Mother," said Jo, "did you go away just to let us see how silly we were?"

"Yes, I wanted you to understand that we can only be happy in the home when each does her part. I thought it would be a good lesson for you to see what happens when no one helps in the house, and you each do only what you like, without thinking of the others. Aren't you all tired of having nothing to do?"

"Yes, we are!" said the girls.

Ten

DREAMLAND

One fine September day, the four sisters had walked to the shaded part of a hill not far from their house. Laurie, who had been very lazy that

morning, found them all working under the trees.
Meg was doing needlework, Amy was drawing, Beth
was gathering pretty-coloured seeds, and Jo was
reading from a book to the others.

They were all so busy that they did not notice
Laurie until he was quite near. Then he said, "May
I come in, please—or shall I be a trouble to
you?"

Meg looked as if she did not want him to come,
but Jo said:

"Of course, you may come in. We should have
asked you before, but we thought you wouldn't want
to join such a party of girls."

"I always like your parties, but if Meg doesn't
want me, I'll go away."

"You can stay if you do something," said Meg.
"It's against the rules to be lazy here."

"I'll do anything you like if you let me stay. I'm
so tired of being alone in the house."

"Then take this book and read to us," said Jo.

Laurie took the book and read it aloud to the end.
Then he said:

"And now may I ask what this new plan is that you
seemed to have started?"

"Shall we tell him?" Meg asked, looking at her
sisters.

"Well," said Jo, "after our first lazy week we each
decided to do a certain amount of work every day.
Mother likes us to be out of doors as much as
possible, so we bring our work here and have very
happy times. We've been pretending that we are
pilgrims, and that dreamland is there, over the hill."

Jo pointed, and Laurie looked through an opening in the wood, across the fields on the other side of the river, to the green hills in the distance which rose to meet the sky. The sun was low, and the clouds were shining in the golden light, like the walls of some wonderful city.

"Wouldn't it be fun if all our dreams came true, and we could live in them?" said Jo.

"I have dreamed so many that it would be hard to say which one I'd most like to come true," said Laurie.

"Well, you'll have to decide," said Meg. "Now tell us which of your dreams you like best."

"I'll tell mine if you will all tell yours."

"Yes," said the girls, "we will. Now, Laurie."

"After I'd seen as much of the world as I wanted to," said Laurie, "I would go to live in Germany, and have as much music as I wanted, and at last become a famous musician myself. I would never trouble about money or business, but I would just live for what I like. That's my dream. Now, what's yours, Meg?"

Meg took a long time before she said slowly, "I should like a lovely house, full of lovely things, nice food, pretty clothes, plenty of money, pleasant people——"

"Wouldn't there be a man in your house?" asked Laurie.

"I said 'pleasant people'," said Meg, not looking at him.

"Why don't you say you'd like a good-looking, wise husband," said Jo, "and some dear little children? You know that your dream house wouldn't be perfect without them."

"Well, *you* would have nothing but pens and paper and books in yours," replied Meg hotly.

"Of course; I should have rooms filled with books, and a pen which would help me to write books of my own—to make me the most famous writer in the world."

"My dream is just to stay safe at home with Mother and Father, and help to take care of the family," said Beth.

"No other wishes?" asked Laurie.

"Not since I had my little piano."

"I have very many wishes," said Amy, "but my favourite is to go to Rome, paint pictures, and be the greatest artist in the world."

"Oh!" said Laurie. "We all want to be rich and famous except Beth."

"I wonder where we shall all be in ten years' time?" said Jo.

"I hope I shall have done something to be proud of by then," said Laurie, "but I'm almost afraid I'm too lazy, Jo."

"Mother says you'll work when you have some good reason to make you work."

"Does she? I hope she's right. I ought to work to please Grandfather, but he wants me to go to college for four years, and then be a merchant and look after his ships. But I don't want that sort of life—I should hate it. If I go to college for four years, that ought to be enough for Grandfather. If there was anyone else to stay with him, I'd run away at once to Germany and my music."

Laurie spoke more angrily than they had ever heard him speak before.

"You ought to do as your grandfather wants, Laurie," said Jo. "If he sees that you work hard now and at college, I am sure he will be kind to you. There will be no one to stay with him if you go away."

That night, when Beth played to his grandfather the simple music which the old man loved, Laurie stood outside in the shadow, and listened. He said to himself, "How lonely Grandfather would be if I went away! I'll let my dream go, and I'll stay with him while he needs me, for I am all he has."

Eleven

THE TELEGRAM

"November is the most unpleasant month in the whole year," said Meg, standing at the window one grey afternoon, looking out at the frozen garden.

"That's the reason I was born in it," said Jo.

"If something very pleasant happens now, we shall all think it is a delightful month," said Beth, who took a hopeful view of everything, even in November.

"Yes," said Meg, "but nothing pleasant ever does happen in this family. We go along, day after day, without a bit of change, and with very little fun."

"You *are* sad, poor dear!" cried Jo. "And I'm

not surprised, for you see other girls having a lovely time, while you do nothing but work, work, from one year's end to another."

Beth, who was still looking out of the window, said, smiling, "Two pleasant things are going to happen: Mother is coming down the street, and Laurie is coming through the garden as if he had something nice to tell us."

Mrs. March and Laurie came in together. A few minutes later there was a ring at the front door, and Hannah came in with a letter.

"It's one of those nasty telegrams," said Hannah, as if she was afraid that it would explode in her hand.

Mrs. March turned white as she took it, and when she had read it she fell back, with a cry, in her chair.

Jo took up the telegram and read:

> *Mrs. March,*
>   *Your husband is very ill. Come at once.*
> *S. Hale,*
> *Blank Hospital, Washington.*

For a few minutes everyone was silent. Then Mrs. March said, "I shall go at once, but it may be too late. Oh, children, children, help me to bear it!"

The girls gathered round their mother as she held out her arms to them. For a few minutes they all wept, until Hannah dried her tears and said, "I won't waste any more time in crying. I'll go and get your things ready for your journey."

"She's right—there is no time for tears now," said Mrs. March. "Stop crying and let me think over my plans. Where is Laurie?"

"I am here," said Laurie. "What can I do to help?"

"Send a telegram to say that I will come by the morning train."

"I'll go at once," said Laurie. "Is there anything else I can do?"

"You can leave a note for Aunt March. Jo, bring me a pen and some paper."

Jo knew that her mother was writing to Aunt March to ask for money for the journey. "How I wish," she thought, "that I had some money to give her."

"Now, Laurie," said Mrs. March, "here is the letter. You need not ride too fast as I cannot travel until tomorrow morning. Jo, go and buy these things which I shall need for your father. Beth, go to Mr. Laurence and ask him for some wine—I can ask anything for you now. Meg, come and help me find my clothes for the journey."

For a short time they were all too busy even to cry. Then Meg asked her mother to rest for a little time while she made her some tea. As she was doing this, old Mr. Laurence came back with Beth.

"Beth has just told me about your husband's illness; it is very sad news," he said. "Here is the wine which you asked for, and I have brought these other things which may perhaps be useful. You may be sure that, while you are away, I shall do all that I can to help the girls. But do you feel able to go on this long journey alone? Would you allow me to come with you?"

Mrs. March looked for a minute as if she would

be glad for him to come, for she was rather afraid of the long journey alone; but she soon decided that she could not allow the old man to go so far. She told him so, with the warmest thanks for his offer. He walked away, saying that he would be back soon.

Meg was bringing a cup of tea to her mother when she was surprised to meet Mr. Brooke.

"I have heard the sad news of your father's illness, Miss March," he said in a kind and quiet voice, which sounded very pleasant to Meg. "I am going to Washington for Mr. Laurence," he went on, "to buy some things which he needs there, and I have come to ask if Mrs. March will allow me to go with her. I shall be so glad if I can give her any help."

"How kind you are!" said Meg. "Mother will be very pleased, I am sure; and we shall all be glad to know that she has someone to take care of her."

Meg spoke as if in a dream, and, she forgot herself entirely until something in the brown eyes looking down at her made her remember the cooling tea, and lead the way into the sitting-room, saying that she would call her mother.

Everything was arranged by the time that Laurie came back with a letter from Aunt March. It was not a very kind letter, but it enclosed the money for Mrs. March's journey. Jo had not yet come back, and they were all beginning to wonder what had happened to her. At last she walked in, put twenty-five dollars into her mother's hands and said, "This money is for Father—to help him in his illness and to bring him home."

"My dear, where did you get it?" asked Mrs. March. "I hope you haven't done anything foolish —or wrong."

"No, I didn't steal it," said Jo, in a rather troubled voice. "I only sold what was my own." As she spoke she took off her hat, and they all cried out when they saw that her hair was cut short.

"Your hair! Your beautiful hair!"

"Oh, Jo, how could you?" cried Mrs. March.

She seemed unable to say any more, but she looked at Jo in a way which made Jo feel that what she had done had been worth doing.

That night, when they were all in bed, Amy and Beth were soon asleep. Meg thought that Jo was also asleep, until she heard a sound of quiet weeping.

"Jo, dear, what are you crying about?" she asked.

"My—my hair!" said poor Jo, trying to stop her tears. "But I'm not sorry," she said bravely. "I'd do it again tomorrow if I could."

Twelve

ILLNESS

Breakfast was very early next morning. It seemed strange to the girls to be up at that early hour.

"Children, I leave you to Hannah's care—and dear Mr. Laurence will, I know, be a good friend to you. Go on with your work, and don't lose hope. Work is always a help in time of trouble."

"Yes, Mother."

"Meg, dear, look after your sisters. In any difficulty, ask Hannah or Mr. Laurence. Jo, write to me often, and be my brave girl, always ready to help. Beth, your music will help you, and you have your little home duties; and Amy, I know that you will be good and try to help the others all you can."

"We will, Mother! We will!"

They heard the carriage coming; but although their hearts were very heavy they did not cry. They sent loving words to their father, knowing that he might never hear them. They kissed their mother quietly, and tried to wave their hands happily as she drove away.

At that minute the sun came out, and, looking back, Mrs. March saw it shining on the girls who were standing at the gate with old Mr. Laurence, the good Hannah and the friendly Laurie.

"How kind everyone is to us," she said, turning to Mr. Brooke who was sitting beside her in the carriage.

"Of course they are," he said, "because they all love you." Mrs. March felt that the kindness of the young man would be a great help to her on her long journey.

When the carriage was out of sight, the girls came inside the house and they began to cry. Hannah wisely left them alone for a time. Then she came in with a coffee-pot, saying:

"Now, my dears, remember what your mother

said, and don't cry any more. Come and have a cup of coffee, and then we'll all work, as we promised your mother we would."

They sat round the table drinking the coffee and Jo said, "Hope and keep busy—that's what we must do. Let's see who can remember it best. I shall go to Aunt March as usual."

"I shall go to teach the King children," said Meg, wishing that she hadn't made her eyes so red. "But I'd much rather stay at home and attend to things here."

"No need of that," said Amy. "Beth and I can keep house perfectly well. Hannah will tell us what to do, and we'll have everything nice when you come home."

This made the girls laugh and they all felt better for it.

A few days later a letter came from their mother which made them all very happy. Although their father was still ill, he was getting better. After that, Mr. Brooke wrote every day, and his letters became more and more hopeful as the week passed. Meg, as the head of the family, read these letters to the girls; and soon they were all writing letters to their father and mother and to Mr. Brooke.

For a week the amount of goodness in the old house would have been enough to supply all the neighbours. But, when they knew that their father was getting better, the girls did not try quite so hard to be good, and little by little they fell back into the old ways.

Jo caught a bad cold because she forgot to keep

her head covered up warmly after her hair was cut.
Aunt March told her to stay at home until she was
better, because she did not like to hear a person read
with a cold in her head. Jo liked this, and was glad
to spend the time sitting by the fire and reading all
the books she could find. Meg went every morning
to teach the little King girls, but she spent most of
her time at home in reading, again and again, the
letters sent by Mr. Brooke, and in writing to him and
her mother. Amy forgot much of the housework
which she had promised to do, and she sat drawing
when she ought to have been helping Hannah.

Only Beth kept on working. She did many of
the things her sisters forgot, and she tried to be a
help to everyone. One day she said to Meg: "I wish
you would go and see the Hummels. You know
that Mother told us not to forget them."

"I'm too tired to go this afternoon," replied Meg,
who was resting in a chair by the fire.

"Can't you go, Jo?" asked Beth.

"It is too stormy for me with my cold."

"I thought it was almost well."

"It's well enough for me to go out with Laurie,
but not well enough to go to the Hummels," said
Jo, laughing.

"Why don't you go yourself?" asked Meg.

"I *have* been to them every day," said Beth, "but
the baby is ill, and I don't know what to do for it.
Mrs. Hummel goes away to work, and Lottchen
takes care of it; but it gets worse and worse, and I
think you or Hannah ought to go."

"I'll go tomorrow," said Meg.

"I would go today," said Jo, "but I want to finish my writing. Why don't you ask Hannah for something nice, Beth, and take it round? The air will do you good."

"I am very tired," said Beth. "I did hope that one of you would go."

"Amy will be in soon and she will go for us."

"Well, I'll rest a little and wait for her."

So Beth sat in a big chair to rest, the others returned to their work, and the Hummels were forgotten.

About an hour later, when Hannah was sleeping by the kitchen fire, Beth quietly filled a basket with good things for the poor children. Then she put on her coat and hat and went out into the cold air, with a heavy head and a sad look in her eyes. It was late when she came back, and no one saw her go quietly upstairs and shut herself in her mother's room. Jo found her there half an hour later, sitting on the bed and looking very ill.

"What's the matter?" Jo cried; but Beth put out a hand as if to stop her sister from coming near.

"You've had scarlet fever, Jo, haven't you?" she asked.

"Yes; years ago, when Meg did. Why?"

"I'll tell you," said Beth; and then, beginning to cry, she went on—"Oh, Jo, the baby's dead!"

"What baby?"

"Mrs. Hummel's; it died in my arms before she got home."

"Oh! My poor dear! I ought to have gone,"

said Jo, taking her sister in her arms as she sat down in her mother's big chair. "What did you do when the baby died?"

"I just sat and held it softly till Mrs. Hummel came back with the doctor. He said it was dead, and then he looked at the two other children, and said that they had scarlet fever, and he told Mrs. Hummel that she ought to have called him before. But she said, 'I'm so poor, and I tried to cure the baby myself, but now it's too late, and it's only with the help of others, Doctor, that I shall be able to pay you.' Then he smiled and was very kind, and he looked at me and he gave me some stuff which I must drink so that I may not get the fever."

"No, you won't get it!" cried Jo, holding her close. "Oh, Beth, if you are ill I shall never forgive myself."

"Don't be afraid. I don't think I shall have it badly. I've taken the stuff, and I feel better," said Beth, trying to look as well as she could.

"If only Mother were at home!" said Jo. "I'll call Hannah. She knows about illness."

"Don't let Amy come; she has not had it, and I should hate to give it to her. Are you sure that you and Meg can't have it again?"

"I don't think so, but I don't care if I do," said Jo, "because I allowed you to go to the Hummels in that way, when I was doing my writing at home."

When Hannah came she at once made them both feel happier. "Everyone has scarlet fever," she said, "and no one dies of it if they are treated properly." Jo believed her and she went up to call Meg. When they were together again, Hannah said, "Now I'll tell you what we'll do. We will have Dr. Bangs, just to look at you, dear, and to see that we start right. Then we'll send Amy off to Aunt March for a time, so that she may not catch the fever; and one of you girls can stay at home and help for a few days."

"I shall stay, because I'm the oldest," said Meg.

"*I* shall, because if I had done my duty and gone to see the Hummels, Beth would not be ill," said Jo.

"Which will you have, Beth?" asked Hannah. "We don't need more than one."

"Jo, please," said Beth.

This settled the point, and Meg, feeling a little hurt, said, "I'll go and tell Amy."

When Amy heard that she was to be sent to Aunt March she was angry.

"I don't like Aunt March," she said, "and I don't wish to be sent off as if I am in the way."

"It's only to keep you well," said Hannah. "You don't want to have the fever, do you?"

"No, I don't; but I expect I shall have it, for I've been with Beth all the time."

Just then Laurie came in, and he was soon told of all that had happened. When he heard that Amy did not wish to go to Aunt March, he began to talk very kindly to her.

"Now, Amy," he said, "if you will help your sisters and Hannah by going to Aunt March like a good little girl, I will come to see you every day and I will take you out and we will have lovely times together."

At last, when he had told her at some length about the lovely times they would have, Amy kissed him and said that she would go.

"Now, is there anything else I can do?" Laurie asked.

"Go and get Dr. Bangs," said Meg. "We can't decide anything until he comes."

"He's a good boy," said Jo, watching him jump over the wall as he hurried away.

Thirteen

LIFE OR DEATH?

When Dr. Bangs came he said that Beth had scarlet fever. He thought that she would have it lightly, but when he heard the story of the Hummels he looked serious. He said that Amy should go at once to Aunt March.

Beth soòn became very ill. Dr. Bangs came to see her often, but he was a very busy man and he was glad to leave Beth in the care of the good Hannah. Meg did not go to teach the King children because it was thought that she might take the fever to them. She stayed at home and did housework. When she wrote to Mrs. March she felt that she ought to tell her mother about Beth's illness; but Hannah said, "No, my dear, don't say anything about it; Beth isn't so very bad, and it would be wrong to trouble your mother while your father is so ill."

Mrs. March wrote from Washington that Mr. March was not so well, and that he would not be coming home for a long time. Beth grew worse, and Jo, who attended to her by day and night, was very troubled when she found that Beth did not know her, and that she called the others by wrong names, and often cried out for her mother.

One morning, when Dr. Bangs came, he looked at Beth for a long time, held one of her hot hands in both his own, and then said to Hannah:

"If Mrs. March *can* leave her husband, I think she should come."

Jo, who was standing near, turned white. "I'll send a telegram at once," she said. She hurried off and was soon back again. While she was taking off her coat, Laurie came in with a letter saying that Mr. March was better. Jo read it thankfully, but the heavy weight did not seem lifted from her heart, and she looked so unhappy that Laurie asked quickly:

"What is it? Is Beth worse?"

"I've sent for Mother," said Jo, with a sad look as she tried to get off her heavy shoes.

"I'm so glad," said Laurie. He put her in a chair and pulled off her shoes for her and then asked, "Did you do it yourself, without asking anybody?"

"No, the doctor told us to."

"Oh, Jo, it's not so bad as that, is it?" cried Laurie.

"Yes, it is; she doesn't know us; she doesn't look

like my Beth—and there's nobody to help us bear it."

As the tears streamed fast down poor Jo's face, she put out her hand in a helpless sort of way as if feeling in the dark. Laurie took it in his, saying as he did so—"I'm here, Jo; hold on to me, dear!"

She could not speak, but she did "hold on," and holding the friendly hand seemed to help her.

At last she said, "You are a good doctor, Laurie, and such a good friend."

"I think that tonight I shall bring you something that will do you even more good," said Laurie.

"What is it?" cried Jo, forgetting her sadness for a minute in her wonder.

"I sent a telegram to your mother yesterday, and Brooke answered that she would come at once. She will be here tonight. Aren't you glad I did it?"

"Laurie, you're a dear! How shall I ever thank you? But what made you think of it?"

"Well, you see, I got rather troubled, and so did Grandfather. We thought that Hannah was wrong in saying that your mother must not be told about Beth—and we didn't like what we heard about Beth; we thought your mother ought to know. So we sent a telegram; and your mother is coming by the train which gets here at two o'clock. I shall go and bring her to you."

"Oh, Laurie, I'm so happy!" said Jo as he went away.

Jo then went to tell Hannah and Meg the good news that Mr. March was better, and that Mrs.

March was coming home.

Dr. Bangs came, and after looking for some minutes at Beth, he said:

"She is very near the time when there will be a quick change—either for better or worse. I will come again later." The girls never forgot that night. They had no sleep, for they kept watch in Beth's room, with the sad feeling of being powerless which comes to us in hours like these.

Midnight came. Then another hour went by and nothing happened except that they heard Laurie starting for the station.

It was past two o'clock. Jo was standing at the window listening for the sound of the carriage; then she heard a movement by the bed, and, turning quickly, saw Meg kneeling by the bedside with her face hidden. She thought, "Beth is dead, and Meg is afraid to tell me."

She went to the bed and saw that the look of pain on the lovely face of her little sister was gone. Beth looked as if she was at peace, and Jo said, "Good-bye, dear, dear Beth; good-bye!"

This waked Hannah, who had been taking a little rest. She came to the bed, looked at Beth, felt her hands, and then cried, "The fever has turned; she's sleeping easily. And now she'll soon be better. Oh, how wonderful it is!"

Before the girls could believe that it was true, the doctor came. He was rather an ugly man, but they thought his face was quite beautiful when he said with a fatherly look at them, "Yes, my dears, I think the little girl will get better this time.

Keep the house quiet; let her sleep, and when she wakes, give her—"

What they were to give they never heard, for they both went out into the dark hall and, holding each other close, wept tears of joy.

"If only Mother would come now!" said Jo.

"Listen!" cried Meg. "I think I hear the sound of the carriage."

The sounds came nearer. Then there was a ring at the door. Hannah opened it, and they heard a call from Laurie, "Girls, she's come! She's come!"

Fourteen

THE MOTHER'S RETURN

Beth woke from a long sleep to find her mother looking down upon her. She was too weak to wonder at anything, but she returned the loving kiss which her mother gave her, and then, without speaking, soon went to sleep again. While Mrs. March sat at the bedside, holding Beth's hand, she told the others all her news.

Evening came. Meg was in the sitting-room writing to her father to tell him of her mother's safe arrival. Jo went quietly to Beth's room where she found her mother in her usual place. Jo walked about the room, looking undecided and not very happy.

"What is the matter, dear?" asked Mrs. March.

"I want to tell you something, Mother."

"About Meg?"

"How did you know? Yes, it's about her. It's a little thing but it troubles me."

"Beth is asleep; speak low and tell me," said Mrs. March.

Jo settled herself on the floor at her mother's feet.

"Last summer," she said, "Meg left a pair of gloves in the Laurences' house; and only one was returned. Laurie said to me: 'Mr. Brooke has got it. He keeps it with his own gloves. Once he dropped it and I made fun about it. Then Mr. Brooke said that he liked Meg but dare not tell her because she was so young and he is so poor.'"

Jo looked up into her mother's face: "Now, aren't you sorry to hear this?"

"Do you think Meg cares for him?" asked Mrs. March.

"I don't know anything about love and all that foolishness," cried Jo. "In stories, girls show it by getting red in the face and growing thin and acting foolishly. Meg does not do that: she eats and drinks and sleeps like anyone else, but she gets a little red when Laurie makes fun about lovers."

"Then do you think that Meg does *not* care about John?"

"Who?" cried Jo.

"Mr. Brooke. We began to call him John in Washington, and he likes it."

"Oh! I know you'll take his part!" said Jo, who felt that this talk was not going to end as she wished it.

"He has been quite open about it. He told us that he loves Meg, but he wants to be able to give her a good home before he asks her to marry him. And I would not allow Meg to promise to marry anyone while she is so young."

"Of course not!" said Jo. "I knew there was trouble coming! I wish I could marry Meg myself

Mrs. March smiled. Then she said, "Jo, I don't want you to say anything to Meg. When John comes back and I see them together I shall be able to see what her feelings are."

"I see it all now," said Jo. "They'll go about the house like lovers, and we shall have to get out of their way, and she will be of no use to me any more. Oh, dear! Why aren't we all boys? Then there wouldn't be any trouble."

Jo looked up and saw the look of sadness in her mother's face. "You don't like it, Mother. I'm so glad! Let's send him away, and we'll all be happy together again."

"I ought not to feel sad, Jo. It is quite right that you should all have homes of your own. But it must be some years before John can make a home for her. I hope that things will go well for her."

"Don't you wish that she would marry a rich man?" asked Jo. "I had planned to have her marry Laurie, and to have plenty of money all her life. Wouldn't that be nice? He's rich and kind and good, and he loves us all."

"Don't make plans for other people, Jo. Time and their own hearts will make your friends' marriages. Making such plans may spoil your friendships."

"Well, I won't. But I hate to see things going wrong when a pull here and a cut there would straighten them out. I wish there was something one could drink to stop one growing up."

Meg came into the room with the finished letter in her hand.

"It's beautifully written," said Mrs. March, looking at the letter. "Please add, 'Mother sends her love to John.' "

"Do you call him John?" asked Meg, smiling.

Fifteen

THAT BAD BOY

In the next few days Laurie discovered that Jo had a secret. He did his best to make her tell him what it was. Very soon he saw that it was about Meg and Mr. Brooke, and he made up his mind to have some fun with them.

Meg herself was acting rather strangely.

"Meg is in love," said Jo to her mother. "She doesn't eat much, she lies awake at night, and she goes off by herself. What shall we do about it?"

"We can do nothing but wait and be kind to her, until father comes back to put things right," said her mother.

A little later, Jo was handing out letters from the post-box. "Here's one for you, Meg," she said.

The next minute there was a cry from Meg.

"What is it, my child?" asked her mother, while Jo took the letter from Meg and read it.

"It's all a mistake," said Meg. "John Brooke didn't send this. Oh, Jo! How could you do it?" And Meg hid her face in her hands and cried as if her heart was broken.

"Me! I've done nothing. What is she talking about?" cried Jo, surprised.

Meg looked very angry as she gave Jo another letter: "You wrote this, and Laurie helped you. How could you be so unkind to us both?"

Jo and her mother read the letter:

My dearest Meg,

I can no longer wait to tell you how much I love you. I dare not tell your mother and father yet, but I think they would let us marry if they knew that you loved me too. Mr. Laurence will help me to get some well-paid work, and then, my sweet girl, you will make me happy. I beg you to say nothing to your family yet but to send one word of hope through Laurie to

Your loving John.

"Oh, that bad boy!" Jo began.

"Jo, are you sure that you did not help Laurie with this letter?" asked her mother.

"Indeed, Mother, I did not help. I never saw that letter before; I should not have written such a silly letter."

"The writing is like John's," said Meg.

"Did you reply to the letter?" her mother asked.

"Yes, I did," said Meg.

"What did you write?"

"I wrote that I was too young to do anything about his letter, or to have secrets from you, and that he must speak to my father."

Jo and her mother smiled.

"You have been very wise," said Jo. "Well, Meg, what did he write after that?"

"In this letter which Jo has just brought, he says that he has never written me such a love letter, and that he is very sorry that my bad sister, Jo, has tried in this way to make fun of us."

Jo picked up the two letters and read them through carefully: then she said quickly:

"I don't believe John Brooke ever saw these letters. I think that Laurie wrote them both, and that he still has Meg's letter."

"Go and bring Laurie at once," said her mother to Jo. "I shall find out what he has done, and see that he does nothing of the kind again."

While Jo was gone, Mrs. March tried to find out what Meg's feelings were about John. "Do you love him enough to wait for him?" she asked.

"I am so angry that I don't want to think about loving any man for a very long time—perhaps never," replied the usually gentle Meg.

Meg ran out of the room as she heard Laurie come into the house with Jo. Mrs. March looked so serious that Laurie saw that she knew what he had done. She spoke to him alone for a long time. The two girls did not know what she said, but when Laurie came out of the room he was very solemn, and they knew that he would never forget what had been said to him.

"I'll never tell Brooke till my dying day," he said to Meg, "and I do hope that you will forgive me."

"I will try," said Meg, "but it was a very wrong thing to do."

He looked so unhappy that Meg and her mother forgave him. Only Jo had nothing to say to him. When she did not speak, he bowed to her, turned round and went home.

As soon as he had gone, Jo wished that she had been kinder, and in a few minutes she set off for the big house to tell him so. She asked at first for his grandfather.

"Is Mr. Laurence in?" she said to the servant.

"Yes, miss, but I don't think he will see you."

"Why not? Is he ill?"

"Oh, no, miss, but Mr. Laurie has made him angry, and I dare not go near him. Mr. Laurie has shut himself in his room and won't answer when I speak to him. Dinner is ready and they don't come to eat it!"

"I'll go and see what the trouble is," said Jo. She went to Laurie's room and spoke to him through the door. Laurie called out, "Stop that, or I'll open the door and make you stop!"

Jo spoke again, and when the door opened she ran in. She saw that he was really angry, and so she went down on her knees and said, "Please forgive me. I came to be friends again."

"Oh, get up and don't be silly," said Laurie.

"Grandfather has just shaken me, and I won't bear it. If anyone else had done it—"

"I don't think anyone else will dare to do that if you look as angry as you do now. Why did he shake you?"

"Because I wouldn't tell him why your mother sent for me. I promised her that I wouldn't tell anyone about those letters I wrote. He was very angry and shook me. Then I was angry too, and I ran up to my room."

"But he didn't know that you had made a promise. I think you ought to go back and tell him that you wish you had not done what gave us all pain—though you cannot tell him what it was."

"No, I won't!"

"Now, Laurie, don't be silly. You can't stay here in your room for ever."

"I don't mean to stay. I shall run away and see the world—and enjoy myself."

"If I were a boy," she said, "we would run away together and have a wonderful time, but it wouldn't be right for a girl. I want you to make friends with your grandfather. If I get him to say he has forgiven you, will you promise not to run away?"

"Yes, but he won't do it—even for you."

Jo went at once to the old gentleman's room. He said, "Come in," in an angry voice.

"It's only Jo, sir," she said. "I've come to bring back a book and ask for another."

He looked at her as if he knew that this was not her real reason for coming.

"What has that boy been doing?" he asked. "Your mother sent for him, so I am sure that he has done something very wrong. What is it?"

"He did do wrong," said Jo, "but we have forgiven him, and after what he has said to us we are all sure that he will not do the same thing again. We all promised not to tell what he had done."

"That won't do," said Mr. Laurence. "I wish to know whether he has been in any way unkind to your mother. If he has, I must beat him."

"No, he has done nothing to my mother," said Jo. "She does not wish anyone to know what happened, and Laurie promised her that he would not tell anyone. That is why he could not tell you, sir, and I hope that you will forgive him."

"Well, if that is so, I suppose I must," said Mr. Laurence; "but he often makes me very angry, and I don't know how things will end if we go on in this way."

"I'll tell you, sir," said Jo. "He will run away."

At this Mr. Laurence looked very troubled.

"Very well! Go and bring him down to dinner," said Mr. Laurence.

"But he won't come, sir. He is so angry because you said that you did not believe him when he said that he could not tell. And I think the shaking hurt his feelings very much."

Mr. Laurence tried to look serious, but Jo laughed. She knew that she had won her point.

"I think if you write him a letter, saying that you now know that he promised my mother not to tell what he had done—and that you would not have shaken him if you had known this earlier—he will see how foolish he had been, and he will come down."

Mr. Laurence laughed again, and wrote the letter in such words as one gentleman might use to another after a really serious quarrel.

Jo kissed the top of his head. She took the letter, ran up to Laurie's room and put it under the door. She waited while he read it. Then he opened the door and said, "What a good fellow you are, Jo! Was grandfather very angry with you?"

"No; hardly angry at all."

"Well, I seem to have been in trouble with everyone. Even you would not forgive me."

"Go and eat your dinner with your grandfather," said Jo.

Everyone thought that this was the end of the matter; but Meg remembered. She never spoke of John Brooke, but she thought of him often, and dreamed of him more than ever.

Sixteen

A HAPPY CHRISTMAS

After her mother's return, Beth got better every day. A small bed was put in the sitting-room for her, and she was able to lie there during most of the day, enjoying the company of her mother and sisters and her much-loved cats.

The news from Washington was good. Mr. March was getting better. John Brooke was still with him, and he wrote to say that they hoped to come home early in the New Year. So the March family were expecting a very happy Christmas, and with Laurie's help they made plans for having a great deal of fun.

"I am so happy," said Beth, "that if only Father was here I couldn't possibly be any happier."

"And so am I!—And so am I!" said all the others.

Sometimes in this strange world, things happen just as they do in story-books; and it was so with the March family on this wonderful Christmas Day.

The girls and their mother were looking very happily at the Christmas presents which they had given to one another and those which had come to them from the Laurences next door. While they were doing this, Laurie opened the door and quietly put in his head.

"Here's another present for the March family," he said in a strange voice.

Then he opened the door wider, and in his place a tall man appeared—so much covered up that his face could not be seen. Behind him was another tall man, who tried to say something but did not seem able to speak.

The first tall man uncovered his face and, with cries of delight, the girls saw that he was their father. It is not possible to tell of all that happened afterwards. The girls and their mother put their arms round Mr. March and kissed him. Quite by mistake, the second tall man—Mr. Brooke—kissed Meg. Hannah came from the kitchen to join in the general happiness, and to tell them that the Christmas dinner would soon be ready.

Mrs. March said to her husband, "Before we have dinner, you and Beth must have a little rest." She put each of them into a big chair, but Beth did not stay long in her own chair; she joined her father in his chair, and they did not have as much rest as they ought to have done because they could not stop talking to one another.

Laurie and his grandfather and Mr. Brooke all came to dinner, and it was a very happy party. After dinner the visitors went away, for they knew that the March family would like to be alone together, and also that Beth and Mr. March needed rest.

That evening the little family was gathered round the fire in the sitting room. Mr. March was telling them how it happened that he came home earlier than they expected.

"When the weather became better," he said, "the doctor thought that I might come—and I wanted so much to surprise you all. I could not have done it without Brooke. He has been such a help on the journey—and, indeed, all through my illness, as your mother knows."

"Yes, indeed," said Mrs. March, "he is a most kind and helpful young man."

There was a happy, far-away look in Meg's eyes. "Such a happy Christmas," she said, "and it has been such a happy year."

"How *can* you say that it was a 'happy year'?" said Jo. "There was Father's illness, and then Beth's illness—and all sorts of nasty things."

"I think that a lot of nice things have come to us this year," said Beth. "We've got to know Laurie and his grandfather, and I've played on the big piano next door, and I have a dear little piano of my own."

"And you went to the Hummels, and the baby died in your arms, and you got scarlet fever, and nearly died of it," said Jo.

"It was rather a hard road for you all to travel," said Mr. March, "and the last part of it was certainly very hard; but from all that your mother has told me I know how well you have done, and I am proud of my little women."

Meg was sitting beside him. He took her hand in his, and he noticed that her fingers had become hard with needlework.

"Meg, my dear," he said, "I know how much work you have done to help your mother and sisters, and I am proud of this little hand. I hope that there will still be some time before I am asked to give it away." He smiled down upon her and pressed the hand which he wanted so much to keep near him. Meg tried to look as if she did not know what her father meant, but she did not do it very well, and she knew that Jo was looking at her rather sadly.

Beth said quietly in her father's ear, "Say something nice about Jo. She has tried so hard, and she has been so very kind to me."

"Although Jo's hair is so short," said Mr. March,

"she does not seem to be so like a boy as she was when I went away. I don't think she wants to be a boy any more. She is more careful about her dress, and she doesn't shout about the house as boys do. In fact she has become a nice quiet little woman! I rather miss my wild girl, but if I get in her place a strong, helpful, kind-hearted woman I shall be very happy. I couldn't find anything beautiful enough to be bought with the twenty-five dollars she sent me."

"And now what have you to say about Beth?" asked Amy. She badly wanted to hear what he would say about herself, but she was willing to wait.

"There is so little of her," said Mr. March, "that I do not know what to say. She might easily hide away so that we could not see her; but I do not think that she is quite so afraid of showing herself as she was." Then he remembered how nearly he had lost her. He held her close, and said with his face against hers, "I've got you safe, my Beth, and I mean to keep you now," He then looked down at Amy, who was sitting at his feet. He passed his fingers through her shining hair as he spoke: "I think that Amy is rather tired, for she has been running about for her mother all the afternoon. She wishes to be useful, and does not now think so much about being beautiful. That is a better way of making life beautiful, for herself and others."

They were all silent for a time. There was a dream-like look on Beth's face, and Jo said to her:

"What are you thinking of, Beth?"

"I was thinking," said Beth, "of that day when we all went up the hill, taking our work with us, and we looked at the hills beyond the river, to the sun shining behind the golden clouds. Laurie joined us, you will remember, and we all talked about our dreams for the future. Now, isn't this like one of our dreams come true?"

"I think it is," said Jo.

Seventeen

JO AND MEG

On the next day Mr. March sat in a big chair in the sitting-room, and the girls spent much of their time with him; now that their father was home again they felt that they could not see too much of him. They looked out at the snow-man which Jo and Laurie had made, and some of them were surprised that neither Laurie nor Mr. Brooke came in to see them. Mr. and Mrs. March often looked at Meg, as if they were thinking a great deal about her and the young man next door. They thought that something must happen soon. This state of uncertainty was not good for the little family, and Jo could see very plainly that it was not good for Meg.

Meg did not look very happy. It was clear that one of her dreams had not yet come true.

"What is the matter with us all?" she said.

"You know very well what is the matter," said Jo.

"It is your John who is causing all this trouble."

"Don't say 'my John'; it isn't right and it isn't true," said Meg, but she spoke the words "my John" as if they were not entirely unpleasant to her. "I've told you I don't care much about him. We are just friends, and now that he is back again we shall all be as we were before."

"I don't think we can," said Jo. "You are not like yourself. You seem so far away from me. I can see what has happened, and so can Mother. When it comes I can bear it like a man, but I wish it was all settled; I hate waiting. If you wish to do it, do it quickly and get it over."

Meg had some needlework in her hand. She was looking at it carefully, and seemed to be very busy. At last she said softly, "I can't do or say anything if he does not speak. And I don't think he will speak, because Father told him that I was too young to be married."

Meg looked as if she was not sure that her father was quite right on this point.

"If he does ask you to marry him," said Jo, "do you know what you will say? Will you tell him plainly that Father thinks you are too young, or will you go red, and begin to cry, and at last fall into his arms, just as people do in the story-books?"

"I'm not as weak and silly as you think," said Meg. "I know exactly what I am going to say. I have planned it all so that I shall not be taken by surprise."

"Would you mind telling me what you will say?" asked Jo.

"Well," said Meg, "*if* he speaks—and, as I've told you, I don't think he will—I shall say 'Thank you, Mr. Brooke, it is very kind of you; but Father says that I am too young at present to think of such things, and I quite agree with him. So please do not say any more, but let us be friends, just as we used to be.'"

"I don't believe you will ever say that," said Jo, "and if you do, I am sure that he will not believe you. He will do just what lovers always do in the story-books, and then you will fall into his arms, if only because you don't want to hurt his feelings."

"You may learn a lot from the story-books you read," said Meg, "but you are quite wrong about John and me. I shall say exactly what I have told you. And then I shall stand up, and bow to him, and walk quickly out of the room."

Meg had no sooner said this than they heard the front door open, and a voice speaking in the hall. It was the voice of John Brooke.

Eighteen

MEG, JOHN BROOKE AND AUNT MARCH

Meg and Jo both rose to their feet as the door of the sitting-room opened and the young man of whom they were talking stood before them.

"Good afternoon," he said. "I come to ask about your father. I do hope that he is not too tired after the long journey?"

"He is resting," said Jo, "but I am sure that he would like to see you. I will go and tell him that you are here."

"Don't wake him if he is asleep," said John Brooke.

"I expect he is reading," said Jo, and she went away quickly, leaving Meg and John alone together.

"Now we shall see what will happen," she thought. "I'm not going to be in any hurry to tell Father that he is here. I'll give them time to have a nice talk. We shall all feel better when we know what they are going to do."

As soon as Jo had gone, Meg also began to move towards the door.

"I am sure that Mother would like to see you, Mr. Brooke," she said. "Please sit down, and I will go and call her."

John Brooke looked very hurt.

"Don't go, Meg," he said. "Are you afraid of me?"

He had never called her Meg before, and she was surprised to find how sweet it was to hear him say it. As she wished to appear friendly and easy, she put out her hand and said:

"How can I be afraid of you when you have been so kind to Father? I only wish I could thank you for it."

"Shall I tell you how you can thank me?" asked Mr. Brooke. He was holding her small hand in his own, and looking down at her with so much love in his brown eyes that her heart began to beat very fast. She felt that she must run away, but also she wanted very much to stay and hear what she knew that he was going to say.

"Meg, dear," he said, "I love you so much. Do you think that you can love me a little in return?"

Somewhere at the back of her mind Meg knew that this was the time for her to say to Mr. Brooke exactly what she had told Jo that she meant to say. She knew also that, after speaking those words, she ought to bow to him, and walk quickly from the room. But her hand was still in his, and all that she could say was:

"Oh, please don't. I'd rather not."

She spoke so softly, and her head was so low, that he had difficulty in hearing the foolish little reply.

"I don't want to trouble you," he said, "I only want to ask whether you care for me—just a little."

"I—I don't know," she said.

Strangely enough, he seemed quite pleased with this reply. He smiled at her and said:

"Will you try to find out? I want to know so much. If you think that you can love me, I shall work hard for us both; but I can't do that unless I know what the end will be."

Meg saw that he was smiling, and a strange thought came into her mind, for she remembered some words that Anne Moffat once said to her. "It's best not to let young men think that they can do what they like with us," Anne said. "Make them wait a little, and then you will have more power over them later on."

Her hand was still in his, but she pulled it away. "I can't tell you anything," she said. "Please leave me alone and go away."

"Do you really mean that?" asked John Brooke. The smile had now quite passed away from his face and he looked very unhappy.

"Yes, I do; I don't want to be troubled about such things. Father says I need not; I am too young, and I'd rather not say any more."

"Mayn't I hope that, some day, you will change your mind? I'll wait, and say nothing until you have had more time. Don't play with me, Meg. I didn't think you would do that!"

He stood looking at her so sadly, and with so much love in his brown eyes, that Meg could not help feeling that she had been unkind to him. He moved towards the door, and Meg followed him. Then the door opened and a new visitor appeared.

"Aunt March!" cried Meg—for she could not have been more surprised if it had been a fairy or Father Christmas.

Aunt March stood in the doorway, looking first at Meg and then at the young man. The young man was very pale and the young woman was very red. It was not difficult to see that the talk which they had been having was of unusual importance to them both.

"What's all this?" cried the old lady, striking the table with her stick.

"It's Father's friend," said Meg. "I'm so surprised to see you, Aunt March!"

"I can see you are surprised," said Aunt March,

sitting down. As she did so, John Brooke went out quietly, saying something about going to see Mr. March.

"Who is he?" asked Aunt March. "Your father's friend; what friend?"

"Mr. Brooke," said Meg. "The friend who was so kind to Father when he was ill. He went to Washington with Mother when the telegram came, and he stayed with Father all the time he was there, and brought him home on Christmas Day. I do not know what we should have done without him."

"Ah, now I remember," said Aunt March. "Brooke—young Laurence's teacher. Are you in love with him?"

"Don't speak so loud," cried Meg. "He may hear. Shall I go and call Mother?"

"Not yet. I've something to say to you and I must say it at once. Now, tell me, do you mean to marry this young man? If you do, not one penny of my money will ever go to you. Remember that, and don't be a silly girl."

This was exactly what was needed in order to drive away the foolish thoughts which had entered Meg's head when she felt that John Brooke was too sure of her. She no longer wished to make him unhappy, or to gain power over him, for she knew now how much she loved him.

"I shall marry whom I please, Aunt March, and you can leave your money to anyone you like," she said, with spirit.

Aunt March looked very angry. "You'll be sorry, miss," she said, "when you've tried love in a very small house, and have found that it won't work."

"I'm not afraid of being poor," cried Meg. "I've been very happy so far, and I know I shall be happy with him, because he loves me, and I——"

Meg stopped there, for just then she remembered that she had not made up her mind—that she had told "her John" to go away; and that perhaps he was quite near, and was hearing all that she and her aunt were saying.

There was something in the girl's happy face which made Aunt March feel that, although she herself was rich, she was a poor old woman living alone.

"Well, I will have nothing more to do with you," said Aunt March. "You are a very silly girl, and you have lost more than you think by what you have said to me. I came to see your father, but I don't feel that I want to see him now. I'm going home, and my last words to you are—I've done with you for ever. Don't expect any help from me when you are married to your Mr. Brooke. Let his friends take care of you. You will get nothing from me."

Aunt March spoke so loud that she could be heard all over the house. She then went to her carriage which was waiting for her in the street, and drove away in great anger.

When Meg was left alone she did not know whether to laugh or cry. She was not given much time in which to make up her mind, for the next minute John Brooke came in.

"Oh, Meg," he said, "I couldn't help hearing— and I am so glad that I heard what you said to the old lady. How brave and good you were! And you *do* love me a little, Meg! You meant what you said?"

"I didn't know how much I loved you until Aunt March said those things about you," Meg began.

"And I needn't go away, but I can stay and be happy, may I, dear?"

Now here was another chance for Meg to speak the words which she had prepared so carefully—the words which she told Jo that she would say to Mr. Brooke before bowing to him and walking from the room.

But she did nothing of the kind, for—just as Jo expected—she said "Yes, John," and then she allowed John to take her in his arms and kiss her.

When Jo came down she found them both sitting in the same chair, and she knew at once that all was lost.

Meg jumped up, looking both proud and happy. John Brooke laughed and kissed Jo—to her great surprise.

"Let us have your good wishes, Sister Jo," he said.

Jo threw up her hands and ran out of the room without saying a word.

Nineteen

THE END OF THE YEAR

Jo found her father still resting, and her mother and the two little girls with him.

"Oh, Father, please come down quick," she said, "and stop John Brooke from kissing Meg! She seems to like it—and he even kissed me, and asked for my good wishes—as if I had any!"

Mr. and Mrs. March saw at once what had happened. They smiled at one another and went down together. Jo threw herself on the bed and began to cry; but when she stopped for a minute, and told the sad news to Beth and Amy, they did not cry as she expected that they would. They seemed quite pleased for they liked John Brooke, and when they understood that he would now be their brother they thought that it was very nice. Jo got no help from them, so she went to her little room at the top of the house and told her troubles to the friendly mice.

No one ever knew what happened in the sitting-room that afternoon. There was a great deal of talking, and Mr. Brooke surprised his friends by the spirit with which he told them about his plans.

"I'm going to work very hard," he said. "I've got something to work for now, and I am sure that I shall make a lovely home for my dear Meg."

Mr. and Mrs. March already loved him as a son. They knew how good he was, and they allowed him to arrange everything exactly as he wanted.

When they all went in to the evening meal, Meg and John looked so happy that Jo felt that she must try to look happy herself, and she did her best.

"You can't say that nothing pleasant ever happens now, can you, Meg?" said Amy.

"No, I'm sure I can't," answered Meg, who looked as if she was living in a dream, lifted far above such common things as bread and butter.

"How full both of unhappiness and happiness the year has been," said Mrs. March; "and how thankful we ought to be that, at the end of it, we are all here, happily together, and with John to keep us company."

"I hope that the next year will end better," said Jo, who found it hard to see Meg with that dreamlike look upon her face.

"And I hope that the year after that will end better still," said John Brooke. He smiled at Meg and added, "I have made my plans and I mean that it shall." He looked as if everything was possible for him now.

"It seems too short a time for me," said Meg. "I've so much to learn before I shall be ready."

"You have only to wait. *I* shall do the work," said John.

"Here comes Laurie," said Jo, who had been looking through the window, and had seen Laurie coming up the garden path with some lovely flowers in his hand.

When he entered the room he went up to Meg, gave her the flowers and said, "For Mrs. John Brooke." Then he offered his good wishes to them both.

"I knew that you would get what you wanted," he said, turning to his teacher. "You always do. When you make up your mind to do a thing, it's done."

"It's very kind of you to say so," said John Brooke. "I thank you for your good wishes and I ask you now

90

to come to my wedding which I hope will be in the year after next."

"I'll come to it even if I'm at the end of the earth," said Laurie. "We'll both be there, won't we, Jo? But what's the matter?" he went on, more quietly. "You don't look too happy."

"It will never be the same again. I have lost my dearest friend," said Jo, who was almost crying.

"You've got *me* anyhow," Laurie answered. "I may not be much good, but I'll stand by you, Jo, all the days of my life; upon my word I will. I shall have finished at college before long, and then we'll go away somewhere and see what the world is like. Wouldn't that please you?"

"I think it would please me, but we can't know what may happen in three years," said Jo.

"That's true. Don't you wish you could take a look forward, and see what will be happening then? I do!"

"I don't think I do," said Jo, "for it might be something sad, and everyone looks so happy now; I can't think that they will be any happier in three years' time. And perhaps they won't be so happy."

Jo's eyes went slowly round the room, looking at the happy faces. Her father and mother sat quietly together, thinking of all that had happened to them both since they first met, over twenty years ago. How much joy they had had together! How much pain they had suffered! And now their four girls were growing up. They were good girls.

"I have no fears for them," said their father. "They will suffer, as we have done, but also I think that they will be very happy.

The father and mother looked at the faces of the young people who were gathered round the fire—Meg and Jo, Beth and Amy, Laurie and John Brooke. "What will happen to them?"

Twenty

THE LITTLE HOUSE

More than a year has passed since the March family, with Laurie and John Brooke, were gathered round the fire on a winter evening, as was told in the last chapter.

John Brooke was working very hard in an office and saving money in the hope that before long he would be able to make a home for Meg. Meg looked prettier than ever. She had spent the time in working as well as waiting, and in learning to do many things which would be useful to her when she married.

Jo never went back to Aunt March, for the old lady had grown to like Amy while Amy was with her at the time of Beth's illness, and she asked Amy to spend her mornings with her. In return, she promised that Amy should have drawing lessons in the afternoons from one of the best teachers in the town. This pleased Amy very much; and it pleased Jo also, for Jo wished to give as much of her time as possible to writing. She wrote stories for the newspapers, and she was very pleased with the dollars which she was sometimes paid for them. Jo also spent much of her time with Beth, who had not been well since her illness. Although not really ill, Beth was never again as rosy and strong as she used to be. Yet she was always hopeful and happy, always busy with the quiet duties she loved, and she was everybody's friend.

Laurie went to college to please his grandfather, and he was having a happy time there. He made many friends, for he was liked by everybody, and he often brought his friends home with him. When this happened, the girls of the March family were asked to meet them.

Amy was the one who most enjoyed this high honour. She was very pretty. She thought so herself, and she was glad when the young men allowed her to see that they thought so too. Meg was thinking too much of her own John to think much of Laurie's young men. Beth had nothing to say to them, and she often wondered how Amy could be so brave as to talk to them as much as she did. Jo also talked to them, and it was clear that they all liked her very much, as she liked them. But none of them fell in love with her, while few escaped some loving thoughts about Amy. It pleased Amy when she saw that they were always rather sad when they went away from her.

Very soon John Brooke had enough money to buy a house for Meg. It was a very small house with a little garden. The garden did not look very well because it had only just been planted with seeds, but

Meg saw it as it would be when the flowers were out. Most of the things in the little house were presents from her family and Laurie. Beth made the cloths for dusting and washing-up. Jo and Amy helped their mother to prepare the house for Meg and her husband. Aunt March sent a large number of very beautiful table-cloths and bed-clothes as a wedding present, but as she had said she would never give Meg anything, she pretended that the present was sent by a friend. Everyone laughed at the way in which she sent a present without breaking the promise which she had made to herself when she was angry with Meg.

At last everything was ready. Meg and her mother went through the house together, and Mrs. March said:

"Do you like it, Meg? Does it seem like home, and do you think that you will be happy here?"

"Yes, Mother, I love it, and I know how much I ought to thank you all; but I am almost too happy to talk about it."

"If only she had a few servants!" said Amy who had just come into the sitting-room after helping Hannah to arrange the kitchen.

"No, Amy," said Meg. "I don't need a servant. I mean to do the work myself, and there will only be just enough to keep me busy—as I wish to be."

"Sallie Moffat has four servants," said Amy.

"Well, she is a rich man's wife," replied Meg, "and she has a large house. In this house there is no room for servants; but I feel that John and I will be very happy here—perhaps much happier than Sallie and her husband in their large house."

While she was speaking, Laurie came in, and a little later, when the others had gone, Jo and he walked home together.

"Perhaps," said Laurie, "you will be the next to marry."

"Don't say such a thing!" cried Jo. "I'm not one of that sort. Nobody will want me, and that's a good thing, for there should always be one unmarried daughter in a family."

"You won't give anyone a chance," said Laurie —and, as he spoke, there was more colour than usual in his sunburnt face. "There is a side of you —at least I hope there is—which you don't like letting a fellow see."

"I don't like that sort of thing," said Jo. "I'm too busy, and I think it's very sad that families should be broken up in that way."

There was a long silence between them, which lasted until they parted at the gate. Then Laurie said, "Mark my words, Jo, you will be the next to go."

Twenty-One

GROWING UP crescendo

The year which passed after Meg's marriage was a very happy one for the March family. Meg often came to see her father and mother as she promised that she would; but towards the end of the year she became the mother of two babies—a boy and a girl. These children were greatly loved by their young aunts, and especially by Beth, who spent much of her time in helping Meg to look after them.

Jo worked hard at her writing, and many of her stories appeared in the newspapers. Amy learned much from the lessons which were paid for by Aunt March: she could now draw very well. Another rich aunt—Aunt Carroll—was so pleased with Amy's work that she offered to take her to Europe. Mr. and Mrs. March were willing that she should go, and Amy looked forward with delight to seeing the pictures painted by the world's greatest artists—for she had already decided that she would be a great artist herself.

One evening, soon after Amy went away with Aunt Carroll, Mrs. March and Jo were sitting together; and Mrs. March said:

"Jo, I want to talk to you about Beth. I am troubled about her." preoccupata per lei

"Why, Mother, what is the matter?" said Jo.

"I thought that Beth has seemed unusually well since Meg's babies came."

"It is not her health that I am thinking of, it is her spirits. I am sure that something is troubling her, and I want you to find out what it is."

"What makes you think so, Mother?"

"She often sits alone. She doesn't talk to me or her father as she used to do, and the other day I found her crying over Meg's babies. This isn't like our Beth. It troubles me."

"Have you asked her about it?"

"I have tried once or twice, but she looked so unhappy that I stopped."

"Dear Jo, you are so strong—and such a help," said Mrs. March. "Now, you will try to find out what is troubling Beth, won't you?"

Jo promised, and for some days she watched Beth very carefully.

One afternoon she and Beth were sitting together. Jo was writing. Beth sat at the window with some needlework in her hands, but her fingers did not move, and soon the work dropped on the floor and Beth looked silently out of the window.

Then someone passed below, and a voice—it was Laurie's voice—called out, "All is well. I'm coming in tonight!"

Beth smiled and waved her hand as the quick footsteps died away. Then she said softly, as if speaking to herself, "How strong and well and happy he looks."

A thought came to—"Beth is in love with Laurie! That is the reason for the unhappiness which Mother has noticed in her. And Laurie makes love to so many girls. He even makes love to me—which sometimes spoils our friendship. But I won't have it. He must love Beth, now that it is so plain that she is in love with him."

Jo lay long awake that night. She was just dropping off to sleep when she thought that she heard Beth crying. She went to Beth's bedside and asked:

"What is it, dear Beth?"

"I thought you were asleep."

"Is it the old pain, that you had after you were ill, that is troubling you again?"

"No, it is a new one; but I can bear it," said Beth, trying to keep back her tears.

"Tell me about it; perhaps I may be able to help."

"No one can help; but lie down here, dear Jo. I'll be quiet, and perhaps we can go to sleep together."

They were soon asleep, but Jo woke early and her thoughts moved very quickly. That morning she said to Mrs. March, "Mother, I want to go away somewhere this winter for a change."

Mrs. March looked up, surprised.

"But why, Jo? And where will you go?"

"I want something new. I feel restless, and I want to be seeing and doing and learning more than I am now. And I've got a plan. You will remember that your friend, Mrs. Kirke, who has a hotel in New York, wrote to ask if you knew anyone who would teach her children and give her some help in the house. I want to write to her and offer my services."

"Are these your only reasons for wishing to go away?" said Mrs. March.

"No, Mother."

"May I know the others?"

Jo looked up and looked down and then said slowly, "Yes, Mother. I am afraid that Laurie is getting to like me too much."

"Then you don't care for him in the way in which it is clear that he begins to care for you?"

"No, Mother. I love the dear boy, as I always have—but not in the way he wishes."

"Have you spoken to Beth?" asked Mrs. March.

"Yes; she would not tell me what her trouble was; but, Mother, I think I know it. I believe that she is in love with Laurie."

"I had not thought that," said Mrs. March, "but it is clear that, for Laurie's sake, you had better go away for a time."

The matter was soon arranged. Mrs. Kirke wrote that she would be delighted to have Jo in her hotel. When Laurie was told that she was going he came to say good-bye to her.

"It won't do a bit of good, Jo," he said. "My eye is upon you; so mind what you do, or I'll come to New York and bring you home."

Twenty-Two

JO IN NEW YORK

New York, November.

Dear Mother and Beth,—I'm going to write you long letters while I am here. I've a great deal to tell, although I'm not, like Amy, a fine young lady travelling in Europe.

Mrs. Kirke is so kind to me that I feel quite at home, even in this big house full of strange people. She gave me a funny little bed-sitting-room under the roof—all she had—but it is warm, and there is a nice table by a sunny window where I can sit and write when I am not teaching Mrs. Kirke's little girls, or helping in the house.

I shall have my meals with the children at present, and I like this better than sitting down at the great table with all the other people in the house. My little girls are pretty children—rather spoiled, I think, but I told them some stories and soon made friends with them.

On the first day I was here I saw something I liked. This house is very high, and it is a long way from the ground floor to the top. I saw a little servant-girl coming up with a heavy load of coal. Then I saw a gentleman, who was coming up behind her. He took the coal from her hand, carried it to the top, and put it down at the door where it was wanted. Then he turned to the little servant, smiled kindly, and said: "It is better so. The little back is not strong enough for such a heavy load."

I thought he spoke like a German, and Mrs. Kirke tells me that he is Mr. Bhaer of Berlin. "He is always doing things like that," she said. "He is very learned and good, but very poor. He is taking care of two little boys, the sons of his sister who married an American and died here. He lives by teaching German and I am glad to let him use my sitting-room for some of his lessons."

Mrs. Kirke's sitting-room has a glass door, and it is close to the room in which I teach my little girls, so that when I pass I can see Mr. Bhaer at his work. I am glad of this, as I like him. But don't be afraid, Mother. He is almost forty, so it is quite safe!

Thursday.

Yesterday was a quiet day. I spent it in teaching my little girls—Kitty and Minnie—and in writing in my own room. I was in the sitting-room last evening when Mr. Bhaer came in with some newspapers for Mrs. Kirke. She wasn't there; but Minnie said to him very prettily, "This is Mother's friend, Miss March."

Kitty, her little sister, added, "Yes, and we like her very much. She tells us lovely stories."

Mr. Bhaer and I both bowed and then we laughed. "Ah yes, Mees March," he said. "I know that you tell them lovely stories, for I hear them laugh. But sometimes I know that these little girls are not good. They do not work as they should—and that hurts you. Now, Mees March, when they are bad like this you must call me and I will come." He pretended to look very cross, like an angry schoolmaster, and the little girls laughed with delight.

I told him that I would certainly ask for his help when I needed it, and he went away.

It happened that I saw him again on the same day, for, when I passed his room, the door was open, and I saw that he was doing some needlework. I felt so sorry that he had no one to do this work for him, but he seemed quite happy, and did not mind my seeing him. He waved his needle at me and laughed.

"I am busy, you see, Mees March," he said.

Jo and Mr. Bhaer soon became good friends. He gave her lessons in German, and he allowed her, in return, to do some of his needlework. It was a pleasant winter and a long one, for Jo did not leave

Mrs. Kirke until June. When the time came for her to go, the children cried, and Mr. Bhaer looked very sad.

"Going home?" he said. "Ah, you are happy that you have a home to go to."

"Now, sir," said Jo, "don't forget that if you ever travel our way, I want you to come and see us."

"Do you? Shall I come?" he asked, with a strange look on his face which Jo did not see.

Twenty-Three

JO AND LAURIE

Laurie worked very hard during his last year at college and he left it with high honours.

When the great day was over, he and Jo walked home together.

"You've done very well, Laurie," said Jo. "I'm proud of you. What are you going to do now?"

"That is for you to decide," said Laurie, in a voice which at once made Jo feel that the moment which she had feared, and which she had wished to put off as long as possible, had come at last.

"Jo," he said, "you must hear me. We've got to talk, and the sooner the better for both of us."

"Say what you like then," said Jo, "I'll listen."

"You must know what I'm going to say," he began. "I've loved you ever since I've known you, Jo. I couldn't help it; you've been so good to me. I've tried to show it, but you wouldn't let me. Now I must have an answer. I can't go on like this any longer."

"I wanted to save you this," said Jo. "I thought you understood——"

"I know you did; but girls are so strange, you never know what they mean. They say 'No' when they mean 'Yes', and drive a man out of his mind just for the fun of it."

"Laurie, you know I'm not like that! You are very dear to me. You're the best friend I ever had; and now you've done so well at college I'm very proud of you. But I can't love you in the way you want me to. I've tried, but I can't."

"Really, truly, Jo?"

"Oh, Laurie, I'm so sorry," she said. "I wish you wouldn't take it so hard. I can't help it. You know that one can't make oneself love anyone—in that way."

"Some girls do."

"I don't believe it's the right sort of love, and I'd rather not try it."

They were silent for some time and then Jo said, "Laurie, I want to tell you something."

He started as if he had been shot, threw up his head and cried, "Don't tell me that, Jo; I can't bear it!"

"Tell you what?"

"That you love that old man."

"What old man?"

"That old German whom you were always writing about—they showed me your letters. If you tell me that you love him—I don't know what I shall do."

Jo wanted to laugh, but she kept herself from doing so, and only said, "Don't be so silly, Laurie. I'm not in the least in love with him, or with anybody. And he isn't old, or anything bad, but good and kind, and—after you—he's the best friend I have."

Laurie looked very sad. "What will happen to me?" he said.

"You'll love someone else, like a good boy, and forget all this trouble."

"I can't love anyone else; and I'll never forget you, Jo, never! Never!"

With that he jumped over the gate and walked quickly away along the river bank.

Twenty-Four

A PARTING

"Now," said Jo to herself as Laurie had passed out of sight, "something must be done about this, and it is I who must do it."

She went to Mr. Laurence and told him the whole story of what had happened. The old gentleman was very kind. He found it difficult to understand how any girl could help loving Laurie; but he knew, even better than Jo, that love cannot be forced, and he decided that Laurie must have a complete change in order to help him to get over his trouble.

Laurie came home very tired. His grandfather

met him as if he knew nothing. They had their evening meal and afterwards they sat and talked as usual, although they both found it difficult to do so.

Laurie seemed so unhappy that at last Mr. Laurence could bear it no longer. He got up, and after walking restlessly for a few minutes about the room, he turned to Laurie and said, as gently as a woman, "I know, my boy, I know."

There was no answer for a minute. Then Laurie asked, almost angrily:

"Who told you?"

"Jo, herself."

"Then there's an end of it," said Laurie, and he looked even more unhappy.

"Not quite," said Mr. Laurence. "I want to say one thing, and then there shall be an end of it. You won't care to stay at home just now, perhaps?"

"I'm not going to run away from a girl. Jo can't stop me from seeing her, and I shall stay as long as I like."

"Not if you are the gentleman I think you are," said Mr. Laurence quietly. And then, with a very kind look in his eyes, the old man went on, "My dear boy, I feel it almost as much as you do. I love Jo, and I hoped that she would become your wife —and my granddaughter. But the girl can't help it. I'm old enough to know that; and I also know that the only thing for you to do now is to go away for a time. Where will you go?"

"Anywhere. I don't care what happens to me!"

"Now, my boy, take it like a man. Most men go through this sort of thing once in their lives. Why not go to Europe as you always meant to do when you left college?"

"But I didn't mean to go alone."

"I don't ask you to go alone. There's someone ready and glad to go with you, anywhere in the world."

"Who, sir?"

"Myself. My business in London needs looking after. I hoped that, when you had some training, you would be able to do it; but I can do it better myself. I shall want you with me in London for a short time, so that you can understand the business when it becomes yours; but don't think that I want to keep you there longer than is necessary. You can go to France, Germany, Switzerland, Italy—anywhere you like, and enjoy the pictures, the music and all the things that you've always cared about."

"Well, sir," said Laurie, "I can't say 'No' to your kindness. I'll come."

Twenty-Five

BETH'S SECRET

The letters which Jo had received in New York had said little about Beth's health, and nothing was said which might lead Jo to think that Beth was becoming worse. The change which was taking place from day to day was not noticed by her father and mother; but when Jo came back, after being away for so long, she saw the difference at once. She knew that Beth was very ill, and as she had saved a little money in New York, she asked her father and mother to allow her to take Beth to the seaside for a few weeks.

This gave great pleasure to Mr. and Mrs. March. They were glad that the two sisters should go away together, and they knew that Jo would take great care of Beth.

They went to a quiet place where there were not many people. The girls made few friends, for they liked to be alone together. They were drawn very close to one another by something of which, for some time, they did not speak—the knowledge that Beth had only a short time to live.

Jo felt quite sure that this was so, and she was glad when, one evening, Beth told her. They had been watching a beautiful sunset, and when at last the sun went down Beth spoke of death—her own death, which she knew must be quite near. For a minute Jo was silent and her eyes were dim. Then she said, "I've feared it, dear Beth, and for some time I've known it, but I'm glad you've told me."

"I've tried to tell you before," said Beth, "but I couldn't. I've known it a long time. At first it was hard to bear, and I was unhappy; but I'm not unhappy now, because I know it's best; indeed it is."

"Is this what made you so unhappy before I

went away?" asked Jo.

"Yes, I gave up hoping then, but I didn't like to tell anybody."

"Oh, Beth, why didn't you tell me?"

"Perhaps it was wrong; but I wasn't quite sure, and no one said anything, so I thought that I might be mistaken. I didn't want to give trouble when so much was happening—Meg's babies, and Amy going away, and you so happy with Laurie— at least I thought so then."

"And I thought you loved him, Beth! I thought that your love for him was making you ill, and it was for that reason that I went away."

Beth looked at Jo in great surprise.

"Why, Jo, how could I, when he was so much in love with you? I do love him dearly, he is so good to me, how can I help it? But he could never be anything to me but a brother."

"Amy is left for him," said Jo, " and they would do for each other very well. But I've no heart for such things now. I don't want to think about anybody but you, Beth. You *must* get well."

"I want to, oh, so much! I try; but every day I lose a little strength, and I feel sure that I shall never get it back. It's like the sun going down, Jo. You can't stop it."

"It shall be stopped," cried Jo. "You're only nineteen and I can't let you go. I'll work and pray and fight against it."

"Jo, dear, it's no good; don't hope any more. Let us be happy together while we can, for I don't have much pain. When we get home, Mother and

Father won't need to be told that I shall not be with them very long, and they will need all the help that you can give them."

She was quite right. No words were needed when the two girls went home. Beth was tired after the short journey and she went at once to bed. When Jo came down she saw at once that her father and mother knew the truth. There was no need for her to tell them Beth's secret.

Twenty-Six

A MEETING AT NICE

While Beth lay dying, Amy was in Rome with Aunt Carroll, and Laurie was in London with his grandfather. For several months Laurie worked hard in trying to learn something of the great shipping business which one day would be his. Then he became restless, and Mr. Laurence felt that he should go away for a time.

"Laurie," he said, "when I asked you to come, I told you that I did not want to keep you here longer than was necessary. You've done well, my boy, and now it's time you had a change. Come with me as far as Paris. I shall be staying with friends there, but they are not the sort of people you would like, and I think that you had better move on by yourself."

"As you wish, sir," said Laurie.

"I have heard this morning," his grandfather went on, "that Mrs. Carroll and Amy March will soon be in Nice. They will be moving on there from Rome. Now Nice is a very pleasant place to spend Christmas. Why don't you go and join them there—after you've had a little tour by yourself?"

And so it happened that on the afternoon of Christmas Day, Laurie was walking down the English Road at Nice—a wide walk, with beautiful flowers and trees on one side, and, on the other side, the sea. Laurie was lost in his own thoughts—not very happy thoughts—when he heard a voice that he knew:

"Oh, Laurie, is it really you! Your grandfather told us that you would be here, but we thought that you would never come."

"I've been wandering about," said Laurie, with a rather tired and unhappy look, "but I said that I would be here for Christmas, and here I am."

"How is your grandfather? Where are you staying? When did you come?"

"My grandfather is well; I am staying at the Chauvain; and I came last night," said Laurie, laughing at Amy's quick questions. "I called at your hotel last night, but you and your aunt were both out. Now tell me, what news have you had from home?"

"Not very good news. Beth is ill; I am afraid she is very ill. I feel that I ought to go home, but they all say 'stay' so I stay."

"I am sure you are right," said Laurie. "You could do nothing at home, and they must all be glad to know that you are enjoying yourself here."

They had now reached the hotel at which Amy and Mrs. Carroll were staying.

"There's a grand dance here tonight," said Amy. "Won't you come?"

A cloud seemed to pass over Laurie's face.

"I don't think I'll come tonight," he said; "but we must meet again before I go. It will be good to talk a little about home."

When Laurie went to Nice he meant only to stay a week, but a month later he was still there. He was tired of being alone, and it was pleasant to be in a place where there was at least one person who came from "home." And Amy, too, was glad to see him, for they could talk together about the people and the places they both loved. Yet Amy was not happy about Laurie. She knew that he was wasting his time, and she felt that, if he was not careful, he would waste the rest of his life. "I must talk to him about it," she thought.

One day, when they were walking together along the shore, she said:

"Laurie, when are you going back to your grandfather?"

"Tomorrow."

"You have told me that twenty times in the last month."

"Well, I have felt that I shouldn't be of much use to him if I went. I hate business, and I'm sure that I shall never be any good at it. In fact I doubt, now, whether I shall ever be any good at anything."

"But you did so well at college. You need not give all your time to the business; I am sure that your grandfather doesn't want that. What has happened to your music?"

"And what has happened to your art?" asked Laurie. "When you went to Rome weren't you hoping to become a great artist? Don't you remember our dreams?"

"Oh, Laurie, when I had seen those pictures, how could I go on hoping then?"

"It seems then that we are both in the same boat, my dear. We are rather lost and don't know what to do with ourselves!"

They were now close to the door of Amy's hotel.

"What I told you was really true," said Laurie. "I'm going back to Grandfather tomorrow. I promise to learn something more about the business, and then I'll begin to think about my music, if you will promise me to think again about your art."

"Good boy," said Amy. "I'll do my best if you will do yours."

They shook hands, and in another minute he was gone.

Amy thought, "How I shall miss him!"

Twenty-Seven

LAURIE AND AMY

Laurie went back to his grandfather, who was now in London, and he spent his days in the shipping office, finding the work much less unpleasant as he came to know more about it. In the evenings he listened to some good music, and he wrote to Amy to tell her of what he was doing. It surprised him that he was no longer thinking quite so much about Jo. He had not written to her for some time. When her answer to his last letter came, it brought him sad news.

"Dear Laurie," she wrote, "It was nice to hear from you but I am so sorry that I have not written before and that my letter must give you pain. Beth is very ill. I spend most of my time at her bedside. I'm glad that you met Amy in Nice. If you write to her, please do not tell her that Beth is worse. We are hoping against hope that when Amy comes home Beth may still be with us. Good-bye, dear Laurie. Please always keep a little corner in your heart for your loving Jo."

She added a little note at the end: "Please write to Amy often. She is very much alone, and your letters will do her good."

"So I will, at once," said Laurie to himself. "Poor little girl. It will be a sad going home for her, I am afraid."

Soon after Laurie left Nice, Mrs. Carroll and Amy travelled slowly towards Switzerland. They were at Vevay when Amy received the sad news of Beth's death. Laurie also heard it in London, and he decided that he would go at once to Vevay and give Amy what help he could. Jo had written that they still did not wish her to come home earlier than had been arranged.

Laurie knew Vevay well. When the boat touched the land he stepped out and hurried along the shore to the hotel where Mrs. Carroll and Amy were staying. He found Amy sitting in a pleasant old garden by the side of the lovely lake. When she saw him she jumped up and ran to him:

"Oh, Laurie, Laurie! I'm so glad you've come."

"I couldn't help coming," he said. "I only wish that I could say something that would help you to bear the loss of dear little Beth."

"You needn't say anything. It is so good to have you here. Aunt Carroll is very kind, but *you* seem like one of the family. How long can you stay?"

"As long as you want me, dear."

Laurie stayed for a week, and each day he and Amy came to know one another better. On the day before Laurie was to leave, they were out on the lake together. Laurie was rowing, and Amy was enjoying the beauty all around her—the mountains, the cloudless blue sky, the bluer lake below and the boats that looked like white-winged birds.

Then her eyes met Laurie's. He had stopped rowing, and he was looking at her so seriously that she felt that she must speak—as if to wake him from a dream.

"You must be tired," she said. "Rest a little, and let me row; it will do me good."

For a moment he seemed not to hear. Then, with a little start, he said:

"I'm not tired; but you may row with me if you like: I must sit near you in the middle of the boat because I'm heavier than you are."

She took the third of a seat which he offered to her, and they rowed together. Amy rowed well, though she used both hands and Laurie used only one. The boat moved easily through the blue water.

"How well we pull together!" said Amy.

"So well that I wish we might always pull in the same boat. Will you, Amy?"

For some time Amy made no reply. They went on pulling together. Then, as the boat touched the shore, Laurie asked his question again, and was answered very softly, "Yes, Laurie."

They were very happy when they returned to the hotel.

Twenty-Eight

ALL ALONE

For some time after Beth's death, Jo was very unhappy. She missed the little sister to whom she had given so much loving care, and with whom she had spent so many hours of every day. She tried to fill her time by working for her mother in the house, and by helping Meg with her babies. She knew that Meg and John were very happy, and she could see that Meg was both a happier and a better woman because she was a wife and mother.

"It is plain that marriage has been good for her," she thought. "I wonder whether it would be good for me; or am I—as I have so often thought—to be alone all my life? Perhaps I'll just watch other people's lives, and put what I see into books, instead of having a real life of my own."

When the news came that Amy and Laurie were to be married, Mrs. March was uncertain of the way in which Jo would take it, and she allowed Jo to see this uncertainty.

"Oh, Mother," said Jo, "did you really think that I could be so selfish and silly as to mind Laurie marrying Amy when I wouldn't marry him myself?"

Jo found that the house-work which she was doing for her mother and for Meg was not enough to fill her life, and she decided to go on with her writing. She went up to the room at the top of the house where, in old days, she and Meg spent so many happy hours. "How long ago that seems," she thought. "We were young girls then, and now Meg is married and has two babies, and Beth is dead, and Amy is going to marry Laurie, and I am left alone."

She decided to look again at the stories she had written and half-written long ago. "I'm older than I was then," she thought, "and perhaps a little wiser because of what I've suffered. If I begin writing again now, I think I know some things which it will be worth while to write about."

She turned to the big box which contained all the stories that she had written, and some old letters which she had forgotten. Among these she found a little note written to her by Mr. Bhaer one evening in New York when he had promised to give her a German lesson, but was afraid that he might be late.

"Wait for me, my friend," he wrote. "I may be a little late, but I will surely come."

"Oh, if he only would!" said Jo to herself. "How good and kind to me he always was! And how I should love to see him; for everyone seems to be going away from me."

Twenty-Nine

A HOMECOMING

Laurie and Amy were married at an American church in Paris. Old Mr. Laurence was so pleased that his grandson was to be married to "one of the girls next door," that he wished the marriage to take place soon—almost as much as the young people themselves. Mr. and Mrs. March made no difficulty, for they thought it right that Amy and Laurie should be married while they were still in Europe, and spend a few weeks there before returning to America. They did not wish to have a wedding at home so soon after Beth's death.

On the day on which Mr. Laurence and the young people were expected home, Mr. and Mrs. March went to the station to meet them and Jo stayed at home to help Hannah prepare a meal. Looking out of the front door, she saw Laurie hurrying up the garden path, as she had so often seen him in the old days. She ran to meet him.

"Laurie! My dear Laurie!" she cried.

"Dear Jo!"

Jo took the hand which Laurie held out to her, and they both knew that a strong and beautiful friendship had taken the place of their childish love for one another.

Soon the small sitting-room was quite full. Amy came in first. "Where is she? Where is my dear old Jo?" she cried. Meg and John Brooke followed, each carrying one of their children. Then came old Mr. Laurence with Mr. and Mrs. March. It was a very happy family party, and no one would have thought that any of them could have been much happier by the arrival of another person. But when the meal was over, and Meg and John had taken their children home, a strange thing happened. The front door bell rang and Jo answered it. A tall bearded gentleman stood before her in the darkness. At first Jo seemed not to know who he was, and then she cried out, "Oh, Mr. Bhaer, I am so glad to see you!"

"And I am very glad to see Miss March," he replied.

"Come in," said Jo; and he was about to follow her when he heard voices.

"But no," he said, "you have a party."

"No, it isn't a party," said Jo. "It's only the family. My sister and her husband and his grand-father have just come home, and we are all very happy together. Do come in and make one of us."

Thirty

UNDER THE UMBRELLA

The business which brought Mr. Bhaer from New York lasted for some weeks, and during that time he came often to see the March family. Then for nearly a week he did not come, and Jo wondered, rather unhappily, what the reason could be.

One afternoon Jo said to Mrs. March:

"Mother, do you want anything in the town? I have to go there to get some paper for my writing."

Mrs. March asked Jo to buy a number of things, and then she said:

"If you happen to meet Mr. Bhaer, bring him home to tea. I quite look forward to seeing the dear man again."

"How good she is to me," Jo thought. "What *do* girls do who haven't a mother to help them through their troubles?"

She bought the paper she wanted, and she was just going to buy the things for her mother when she met Mr. Bhaer. He seemed very happy to see her. "What are you doing here, my friend?" he asked.

"I am buying things for Mother," she said. Just then she saw that it was beginning to rain.

"May I go also, and help carry your things for you; and will you come under my umbrella, for I see that you have none?"

Jo thanked him and they walked on together, both under the same umbrella.

"Why have you not been to see us?" Jo asked. "We thought that you had gone."

"Did you think that I should go without coming to see the friends who have been so kind to me?"

"No, I didn't; but we wondered why you didn't come."

"I thank you all," he said, "and I will come one time more before I go."

"You *are* going, then?"

"Yes; I have no longer any business here. It is done."

"And as you wished, I hope?"

"I ought to think so, for I have found a way to get my bread and to help the two boys—my sister's sons."

"Tell me, please!" said Jo. "I like so much to know about you—and the boys."

"That is so kind. My friends have found a place for me in a college, where I shall teach German."

"That is good news," said Jo. "I am so glad, for we shall hope now to see you often."

"Ah! But we shall not meet often, I fear. The college is far away—in the far west."

It is possible that if Jo and her friend had not been walking under the same umbrella—and there-fore very close together—he might not have seen the tears which she could not keep back. But he did see them.

"Why do you cry?" he asked.

"Because you are going away."

"Jo," he said, "I have not riches and I have not youth; I have nothing but my love to give you."

She took his hands in hers.   "Is not that enough?"

List of extra words

college *place where one may study after leaving school*
doll *small plaything made to look like a girl*
gloves *covering for the hands*
scarlet fever *illness which causes red marks on the skin and a painful neck*
skating *moving on the ice on sharp pieces of iron fixed to the shoes*
telegram *message sent in signs (not spoken) by electricity along a wire or by radio*
quick-temper *a quick-tempered person quickly becomes angry*